THE SAG
BOOK THREE OF TH

Robert Ryan

Copyright © 2020 Robert J. Ryan
All Rights Reserved. The right of Robert J. Ryan to be
identified as the author of this work has been asserted.
All of the characters in this book are fictitious and any
resemblance to actual persons, living or dead, is coincidental.

Cover design by www.damonza.com

ISBN: 9798671260717
(print edition)

Trotting Fox Press

Contents

1. The Blade Master	3
2. For the Seventh Knight	11
3. The Lone Mountain	19
4. A Strange Rider	27
5. Asana	34
6. You are Observant	41
7. A Wise Man is Prepared	48
8. First Training	55
9. The Hundred	64
10. Words of Power	70
11. You are Beyond Good	76
12. Live or Die	83
13. The Lure of the Stone	90
14. Loyal to the King	99
15. Accept Death	105
16. Down the Mountain	112
17. The Shadow of Winter	125
18. The King's Favor	131
19. The Training of a Sage	138
20. Captured	144
21. Death and Magic	150
22. Shadows	159
23. Flight!	168
24. Ancestors	175
25. The Seventh Knight	179
Epilogue	199
Appendix: Encyclopedic Glossary	203

1. The Blade Master

Asana drew his sword, and he felt alive.

The ring of steel against leather as he unsheathed it was his heartbeat, and its song as it sliced the air his spirit. In a sense, the blade was him and he was it. So it had been through the ages, for his forefathers had possessed this same sword, and the souls of his ancestors lingered in the cold metal. He sensed their presence now, as he always did when he drew it.

He felt the weight of the blade in his hand. It was nearly three feet of balanced steel, strong yet flexible enough to bend, sharper than the sting of heartbreak, double-edged and deadlier than a poisonous viper.

Breathing softly, he calmed his mind and relaxed his body for what was to come.

The sword was no ordinary sword. It was a weapon of the nobility, of which he was descended. It was a gentleman's weapon. It was not intended for use on the battlefield, but for personal protection. Yet it had seen battle, heard the clamor of war and slaked its thirst with blood.

Asana stepped forward. His body moved with fluid practice. He no longer needed to think of where to step and how to balance his weight. The grace of the warrior had become his by instinct. If a skill were trained day after day, year after year, it became as natural as the rising sun at dawn.

The blade and the man were one. Steel and flesh twin thoughts born in the same moment and charged by matching destinies.

Yet something was wrong.

He stepped into Otter Swims the Lake, the opening technique of the pattern he had chosen to practice, and he felt a disharmony between mind and body.

As he moved, his mind should have slipped into the detachment of the masters, what was called Calm in the Storm, where no emotion or even thought played across his consciousness. But he did not find it, and that troubled him.

The detachment he sought was a state of mind at his command. It was a sense of existence that acknowledged human emotion, but floated above it, neither fearing anything nor wanting anything. In this manner, the swordsman freed his body to act on trained instinct. He became faster, stronger and more deadly.

But for the first time in years, he could not find that state, and he could not fathom why.

He ceased trying to. Detachment could not be found when the mind puzzled over a problem. Instead, he continued on with the pattern, performing each technique with grace, yet still marking where improvement could be made.

The blade sliced the air. He moved with ease, following the pattern but performing it faster as he went. The sword was a blur, slicing, cutting, stabbing and deflecting. There were few blocks, for this type of blade was not designed to stop an opponent's attack by brute force. That would dull the razor-like edges, even chip the metal. But mostly, it was just not a skillful way to fight.

He recoiled in a defensive move, the sword folding back with him but at an angle to shed an attack in the same manner that rain ran off a pitched roof. Then he sprang forward in a stabbing motion.

The patten had a rhythm to it, for each move gathered energy for the one to follow. Rocking backward in defense gathered his rear leg under him so he could pounce forward with power in attack. A slice to the left was initiated by turning the waist to the left, but having done so, like a corkscrew, the body could pivot to the right with greater strength.

The sword whirred through the air, and Asana's white shoes, light and gentlemanly, moved over the green lawn on which he practiced in a blur.

Faster and faster he went, spinning and twisting, his sword near-invisible as it leaped from one technique to another, and his long tunic of white silk swirled about him.

He danced the game of death, imagining enemies all about him, for that sharpened practice and made it more of a similitude for a real fight, yet still he failed to reach a state of detachment. Despite all his skill, his practice was flawed. Not that many would notice, but he knew and it burned away at him. He sought perfection, and this morning that was denied him.

So he went faster still. Where the pattern should have ended, he commenced again, moving once more into Otter Swims the Lake, but this time in a blur of speed that even the other sword masters he had met would struggle to match. Yet each move remained precise, each angle of the blade exactly positioned. This was the mark of a great master; to achieve correct form at the limits of the body's ability, but there was no pride in him. He was still not as good as he could be. Perfection skittered away like a leaf blown in the wind.

He moved across the green sward, and saw as he did so expanses of land far below. He was atop a mountain, and clouds wreathed it as they often did, but there were many gaps and he saw afar the plain where the river known as the Careth Nien ran. He saw also the green smudge of the massive forest nearby that was known as Halathar, in which the elves dwelt in guarded seclusion.

That world was visible, but it was a different world to his own, and he had not been troubled by it for a long time.

Yet even as he flitted through the pattern, he sensed that was to change.

The mountain retreat had served him well. He was born of a Duthenor father and a Cheng mother, yet he had found no home in either lands where he was fully accepted. Here, though, in self-exile at the top of a mountain, he had found a home. Many years he had enjoyed its peace, but now it was about to be shattered.

He misstepped, and his sword wavered, but he found the rhythm of the pattern again and continued.

His peaceful and near solitary life was over. He had always had the gift of foretelling, and it descended on him now.

The future ran before his inner eye, fleeting images that made little sense, but they would in the days ahead. Some things he saw in detail, and other things were shrouded by mists of uncertainty.

He did not cease to perform the pattern. His body knew what it had to do, and his mind was free to watch the inner vision. Detachment still eluded him though, but now he knew why.

The vision faded, but before it was gone he saw one last scene. A warrior faced him, armored, a mighty sword in his hand and yet not his chosen weapon of death. In the other hand, fire burned. Dark sorcery. And this the knight flung, for Asana recognized him now as one of the fabled Kingshield Knights, and death tore the air and streaked toward him. Too fast it came, and there was no escaping that roaring, leaping fireball that would consume him and end his life.

Mercifully, the vision faded and was gone. Asana came to the end of the pattern. His body felt like ice, and already the dull cold of death seemed to grip him, but in defiance he leaped into Otter Swims the Lake for the third time.

Now, he moved even faster than he had before. Perhaps, he moved with greater speed than he had ever done. Yet still he retained the correct angles and movements, the subtleties within the pattern born of the experience of generation after generation of masters. A slight difference in angle here severed an artery, a slight difference there avoided bone and the tip of the blade penetrated the heart.

He could not capture detachment. The state of Calm in the Storm that he sought was unreachable today, and he knew that it was because he was trying too hard to find it. Yet faced with a vision of his own death, what man, even a master, would not seek to dull the emotions that washed over him?

But he was better than that. He was a master above other masters. He had never been defeated, and even those the Cheng admired and proclaimed as Cheng-mah, warriors of perfection, came to him for tuition, even if they did so in secret.

He danced the great game of death, one with the sword, one with the ground beneath his feet and the mountain on which he stood. Calm in the Storm at last settled over him, and he accepted death. It was a tiny, insignificant thing compared to the vastness of the cosmos. Suns died. Galaxies died. The universe itself hurtled toward oblivion. Yet all had been born and died before. There was nothing new. There was nothing old. Death was but a birth, if only humanity had the perspective to see the pattern of eternity.

His sword stilled, and his body held motionless in perfect balance upon one leg while the other kicked out. For the art of the swordsman was incomplete if it did not also include strikes of foot and hand. To rely on the blade alone was to shun opportunities to surprise an opponent, and no warrior did that. Not one who sought perfection.

Slowly, he sheathed the blade, breathing deep as he did so.

A sense of peace settled deep within him. He would die, but he would die with purpose. There was no shame in having been momentarily scared. There was no shame in wondering if his fate could be avoided.

But it could not. His foretellings were never wrong, and there was no shame either in defeat. For while he would be killed, it would not be by the sword. It would be by dark sorcery, and that was more potent than the greatest warrior.

His glance fell to Kubodin, his faithful retainer. The man squatted on the ground, studying him. A gentleman would have stood quietly to watch, arms clasped behind his back, or sat cross-legged and still on the grass. But Kubodin was no gentleman. He was the opposite of everything that Asana himself was. He was a wild man from the hills. He bathed irregularly, got drunk, swore and wore rags for clothes. He lied and gambled and flirted outrageously with women. Yet Asana loved him, for there was loyalty there stronger than iron, and that was worth more than all the gold in the world. It was more precious to him than the empty, if pretty, words of the nobility who said one thing but thought another.

"Hey," Kubodin said, rising with a grunt and shrugging the brown rags that he called clothes into a semblance of neatness. "What was that? Did ants crawl up your leg? I've seen pigs hold a sword better. You stumbled three times, and twice a man with a bad back and arthritic fingers could have gutted you like a fish. Hey, but what do I know? Maybe that was perfection. Nobles think differently from the common folk."

Kubodin scratched himself vigorously, and then tugged intently at his brass earring as though he did not care what reply might be given.

Asana allowed himself the slightest of smiles. "If you burned those clothes, you would kill the lice that make you itch."

The other man frowned. "The lice aren't enemies. They have a right to live as much as me."

Asana nodded. There was a certain truth to that.

"Hey, so why so bad today, master?" Kubodin persisted.

The image Asana had seen in the foretelling came to his mind once more. The sorcerous fire streaked toward him, and he felt helpless. But he would not burden his friend with foreknowledge of the grief to come. For whatever reason, the hillman had attached himself to him. Supposedly, it was because he had saved the little man from bandits who had surprised and captured him. A life-debt, Kubodin called that. If so, he would soon be released.

"Maybe I'm just getting old and feeble," Asana answered his question. He was only in his fifties, and had never felt stronger, but it would do for a reply.

Kubodin nodded sagely. "Aye, that's likely it. First the body falls apart, and then the mind rots. Never mind, master. After a while you won't notice it happening anymore."

Asana suppressed his smile. This was a game between them. Kubodin always sought to rile him, and he pretended to ignore the other's comments.

The air had been still, but now a breeze began to blow. The weather atop the mountain always changed rapidly, and glancing away he saw that the clouds below were unfurling to tatters. Soon, the sun would burn the remnants away.

"Prepare the halls for guests, Kubodin. There will be three of them."

That seemed to startle the little man, and Asana enjoyed it.

Kubodin adjusted the round leather cap he wore. It was supposed to be armor of a kind, but they both knew it was useless.

"Guests, master? We never have guests."

"We do now, and for a long time." Asana studied the growing gaps in the clouds below. "The world is coming to us, old friend. Things change. Great events begin, and fate has found our little mountaintop."

2. For the Seventh Knight

Menendil swiped a cloth over the surface of the bar. The Bouncing Stone was his inn, and had been in his family for generations. It was a prosperous place, full of regular patrons and passersby. Usually. But times had changed.

The bar was a single slab of polished oak, long and wide. A dark-stained pine cabinet supported it. Legend held that while the cabinet had been replaced many times, the oak bar itself was the original.

He studied it intently, looking for any patch he might have missed. He liked to keep it clean and free of ale spills. Customers liked cleanliness, and he knew how to keep customers happy.

The bar was dented and marked all over. But it was always kept oiled and clean. The age of it, and the age of the inn itself, dating back to the same time as the raising of the Tower of the Stone that was on the street nearby, was his chief selling point. The people of Faladir loved their history, and so while they would hate an ale spill left too long on the bar they loved that it was old and battered.

Old and battered. That was how Faladir itself felt these days. There was a depth of history to this place, and to the city itself. Legend also held that the workmen constructing the tower came here for lunch. That was probably true, for workmen needed hardy food to keep them going, and they enjoyed a pint, or two, of ale as well. But that was not the only legend.

Faladir was founded out of war and strife at the end of the Shadowed Wars. It had been a time of chaos, and some creatures of the Shadow still swarmed the earth.

They had attacked the city. But they were beaten back, their sorcerer king cast down and the Morleth Stone taken and kept safe. But the legend of those times lived on. Elùdraks. Were-beasts. Elugs, and many other creatures of evil that flew, slithered, crawled or walked on two legs like men … but had the hearts of serpents.

Menendil idly folded the bar cloth as he thought. It was true that the folk of Faladir liked their history and legends. But they did *not* like those legends coming to life. Not the dark creatures anyway. But rumor hung over the city like a pall of smoke. Too many people had seen too many strange things for it all to be dismissed. And that was bad for business.

He tucked the cloth into his apron. Had he not seen a dark shadow flying the midnight air and circling the Tower of the Stone himself, maybe he could have dismissed the rumors. Maybe.

But he had seen what he had seen. And others had seen what they had seen. Business had been bad for months, and it was getting worse. Before, the rumors only kept people away at night. Who walked the streets when there was a cry of murder in every alley? But now, even the daytime trade was low.

He looked at his patrons now. It was lunchtime, and he should have been busy. Instead, there was one stranger drinking at the bar, quiet and subdued. In the corner, around a large table near the hearth, sat three people. They worked nearby at the farrier's. He knew them, and he knew they usually laughed loudly and swapped jokes. Today, they leaned close and whispered to each other.

On the far side of the room was another lone man. He too was a stranger, and he had the look of a soldier about him even if he did not wear a uniform. Normally, soldiers were welcome. But not lately. The king had started using them as spies to ferret out those who spoke against what was happening in the city. Not all deaths were blamed on creatures of evil. The king, and those who followed him, were said to be responsible for some of the murders. And those who had been heard voicing opinions had been the first to show up dead, or had disappeared never to be seen again.

The door to the inn swung open, and a tall man entered. A sword hung at his side, and he was cloaked and hooded. But Menendil knew him without having to see his face.

The newcomer looked around, assessing who was in the room and who they were likely to be. His gaze lingered over the stranger on the far side, and Menendil smiled to himself. His friend missed little, and what he did miss was not worth worrying about.

The cloaked man came to the bar and pulled back his hood. Norgril had always had white hair, even when he was young. Blond he called it back then when they were both in the army together, but it had changed little. The only real difference was that his face had now aged to catch up with it.

"An ale, please," Norgril said in a normal voice.

Menendil nodded and began to draw it from the tap. While he did so, his friend leaned in close and spoke softly.

"How goes it, Mender?" He used the old nickname that had stuck since their army days.

"As good as can be expected," Menendil replied quietly. He glanced at the stranger and then looked Norgril right in the eyes.

The other man knew what he was saying. It was not safe to speak freely, and even if what they said when whispering could not be heard it would draw attention to them.

"I'll have one of your meat pies, too," Norgril said. "The beef and ale one."

His voice was loud enough to be heard through the inn, and the conversation, such as it was, normal enough so as not to arouse suspicion.

Menendil placed the pint down on the bar and some coins slid across the polished surface in return.

"There's a batch of pies just cooking out back. I'll check how they're coming on, but they should be just about ready by now."

Norgril moved away from the bar to find a table, and Menendil went through the curtained door that led into the kitchen. His wife was there, just at that moment pulling out a rack of pies from the oven with thick gloves.

"Perfect timing," he said.

"Aye, I heard the order. But mark my words, that friend of yours will get us into trouble. He's one as has the look to him of a child poking a dog with a stick. He can't just walk by and let it sleep."

Menendil knew that was true. "He's the same as me, Norla. We were both in the army, and we both served in an elite unit. It's not in us to ignore what's going on. Our training screams against it."

Norla did not answer that. She was not happy, but she let things be. Norgril was not the first of his old friends to drop by. Instead, she plated the pie, poured on a healthy dollop of sauce from a pot on the stove and handed him the plate in silence.

He knew better than to argue the point now. She did not like his old friends dropping by because she knew it would lead to trouble, but when push came to shove he knew she hated what was happening in their beloved city as much as he did.

He took the plate back out into the main room of the inn, and was surprised. The suspicious stranger was gone, and Norgril sat now where the other man had been. It was a good place, far enough away from the others in the room that if they spoke quietly no one would hear what they said.

Norgril grinned at him, and Menendil placed the plate on the table and pulled back a chair to sit down opposite.

"He must have got bored sitting here and listening to idle chatter," Norgril said. "Either that, or there was someone better to spy on." He took a sip of ale and reached for the pie.

"It's still hot," Menendil warned. "Give it a moment."

His old friend hesitated. Then he looked around the room and leaned in close over the table.

"Have you heard the latest?" he said in little more than a whisper.

"No. No one has been in here yet that I'd talk to."

"Well," Norgril said, "The Shadow Flyers have been seen in broad daylight now. At least over the palace and the city walls. Rumor says it's to discourage people leaving Faladir. They know if they do they'll be found."

Shadow Flyers was a term some folks used for elùdraks, but Menendil preferred the old name that had come down from legend.

"But that's the least of it." His friend took another sip of ale, and there was a hint of outrage in his eyes. Maybe a touch of fear as well.

"What else?" Menendil asked, but he was not sure he wanted to know the answer. He himself had seen elùdraks circle the Tower of the Stone from his own bedroom window in the deep hours of the night. Not to mention strange lights from the small and barred window just below the tower's pinnacle where the Morleth Stone was held. That the creatures of evil were now seen in daylight was even more worrying, but there was obviously worse to come.

"The king tolerates no dissent," Norgril went on. "That we already knew. Murder has become commonplace. But now he's gone further, killing those of his own blood."

Menendil's stomach lurched, and he felt a wave of nausea. He knew where this was going, and it sickened him.

"We know that other members of the royal family have met with accidents. One was killed hunting. Another fell out of bed while he was sleeping and broke his neck. But now murder is no longer even disguised. The last were rounded up last night and executed by sword. All except his youngest brother."

"He escaped?"

"No. He did not. The king thought him the leader of those who would depose him and raise a new king in his stead. The younger brother therefore faced a worse fate than the others."

"What happened," Menendil asked quietly.

"He was found trying to hide in a cellar. The king interrogated and tortured him. Personally. What he said isn't known, but it's doubtful he revealed any plots of rebellion. The royal family have long been watched, so no one would have had any dealings with them. It would be too obvious and too dangerous."

"And after the interrogation?"

Norgril closed his eyes. "He was hung, upside down, from the palace gate. And the king killed him with his own knife, cutting his throat. The body will be left there for a week, I'm told."

It was not really a surprise to Menendil. He had seen this coming. Yet somehow it still shocked him. But he tried to think about it calmly, and what it might mean for the rest of the city.

Things would get worse. That he knew. Evil that was unchecked grew strong and bold. Now that it had removed the greatest threat, someone who might rally men to a banner, it would move on to another target. But there was no target left now who could rally a proper rebellion. The royal line was expunged. The six knights had once been beloved, but they supported the king and there was blood on their hands in service to him. Menendil's own father had been a knight many years ago. Had he been alive now, the shame of what they had done would have killed him.

"How do we know this is true?" he asked.

Norgril looked grim. "I've seen the body, and I had met the prince. It was still hard to identify him though. His face was bloated and bruised from being struck. His body was covered in cuts and blood."

Menendil nodded slowly. His friend had stayed in the army longer than he had. At one stage, he had been a bodyguard to some members of the royal family. There would be no mistake with identification.

"And the rest of the story?" he asked.

"Pieced together from various contacts I still have inside the palace."

The inn seemed even more subdued than it had before. Norgril began to eat his pie, and Menendil sat there and thought in silence.

The royal line was gone. Who then could the city of Faladir rally to for salvation? It was a question that made him uncomfortable. He, like all others, knew the prophecy. The seventh knight would rise to challenge evil. But could one person, alone, defeat the king, his knights, the army that answered to the king and the creatures of shadow that were increasingly seen within the city?

He knew the answer, but he did not like it. The seventh knight would need help. There must be those in the city able to discover information and pass it on. Even, when the time came, to raise their swords in defiance. Either might get them killed though.

But it had to be done. The way must be prepared for the seventh knight. Menendil knew he was not a brave man. Not like his father had been. Yet still, he was not a coward either.

There were others like him too. The plan that he had been considering for some while seemed now the only way forward. He would form a group of those he trusted. He would keep it to one hundred only, so that they had a chance of remaining secret despite the spies who swarmed all over the city. And they would prepare the way for the coming of the seventh knight. Or die trying.

3. The Lone Mountain

Faran gazed ahead. For days, the mountain had grown up before them as they traveled, getting larger by slow increments. Now, it dominated the landscape.

It was larger than anything he had seen. Larger by far than the hills which had surrounded his home village of Dromdruin. It dwarfed even the great escarpment beneath which the tombs of the Letharn had been delved. It was *massive*, but it was still not like any mountain he had heard tell of.

There were no other mountains near it. It was not part of a range. It stood by itself, alone.

He could relate to that. He and Ferla were like the mountain. They were alone. They were the last of Dromdruin Village. But at least they had each other.

They were not quite alone. Kareste was with them, and she had proved a true friend. But she was not of the village. She had not known their world before fire and sword had destroyed it. Yet Faran guessed that she too had endured great pain in her past. She kept it secret though, but the memory of it was there in her eyes and it showed at times. There was a look to the eyes that tragedy engraved, and she had it.

Aranloth must have known her past. She was a lòhren like him. But he was dead. Dead, but not forgotten. His body lay days behind them, buried probably in a tunnel. His grave unmarked and unmourned. He would have fought Lindercroft and his soldiers, but he could not have prevailed against so many.

Faran studied the mountain. Tall it was, the top of it wreathed in clouds. But there was no stony peak stretching up jaggedly into the sky. The mountain was dome-shaped, and the peak was a high plateau of grass, near level from what he had been able to see from time to time. Few trees grew there, but that did not seem to be because it was too high. Even the long smooth slopes coming down to the level of the plain that surrounded it were mostly bare of trees. They were grassed like the plateau, but there were signs of a road spiraling upward.

He heard Kareste coming up beside him. "Does it have a name?" he asked. There was no need to say what he meant by *it*. The mountain dominated everything all around them.

"It has many names," she answered. "But the one most commonly used is that which the Halathrin gave it. Nuril Faranar. The Lonely Watchman."

Faran thought the name suited the mountain. It seemed lonely, yet resolute in its isolation. It had stood through the history of Alithoras, and there was much of that in this region. It was here that his ancestors had gathered together and served the Halathrin. Within its sight, battles had been fought during the Shadowed Wars.

"Is the homeland of the Halathrin close by?" Ferla asked.

Kareste pointed toward the horizon. "It lies that way, though we'll not see the elves who dwell there. But from the top of the mountain, so Aranloth told me, their forest home is visible."

Faran sighed. The mountain was their destination. But it could not be a home as Dromdruin had been, and the valley of the lake after. There was only so much room in his heart, and those places already filled it.

"Will we be welcome there?" he asked.

"There's only one way to find out," Kareste replied. "But it was where Aranloth had intended to take us."

She went silent then, and strode ahead. They followed her, knowing how she felt.

Aranloth was dead. It was too hard to comprehend, but it must be faced. They were doing now what he would have done, and Kareste led them.

Kareste did not know him, but there was a man who lived on the mountain. If forced to flee, it was to this man that Aranloth would have led them himself.

They *had* been forced to flee, but Aranloth was left behind. He had told Kareste of this strange man who lived atop the mountain though. Supposedly, he was the greatest swordsman alive, except perhaps for Brand of the Duthenor. At some point, Kareste claimed, they would have come to him for tuition anyway. Lindercroft had just forced it on them sooner than expected.

They moved ahead, following Kareste. She had changed since Aranloth's death, and though she hid her grief well it was there at all times to see. She was silent most of the time, and her eyes were haunted. The old man was not just another lòhren to her. He had been a friend. Her loyalty to him was enormous, and his loss had changed her.

She usually walked ahead of them, and once Faran had caught up with her to ask a question. She had had tears in her eyes, and he had not known what to say or do. What comfort could you give to the living who grieved the dead?

Yet despite Kareste's grief, she had led them well. They had crossed the lake near the cabin unnoticed by Lindercroft or his men. Then coming to the shore on the other side she had sunk the boat in water deep enough that no trace of it could be seen or found by those who would pursue them when they realized they had not died in the burning cabin.

Using mist and smoke she hid them as they moved on, although it was Ferla who had found the best path for them up out of the valley that would leave little sign of their passing if one of Lindercroft's men was a tracker.

It was Kareste though who led them undetected through the line of sentries atop the ridge that Lindercroft had placed. They had not been vigilant, seeing the smoke from the burning cabin far below and assuming that their leader had cornered his quarry.

She had used mist to hide them, making it seem that it rose up naturally from the lake, and she had deepened shadows also that they flitted through until they were past all danger.

Through woods she led them, and over rocky slopes that hid their trail. And they moved at great speed, resting seldom and pushing themselves to their limits. For elùdraks would hunt for them when Lindercroft discovered they had escaped him.

These things had worked, and the time Aranloth had bought them with his life proved invaluable. They had seen no sign of the enemy, either on land or in the air, and they had traveled for a week. Two hundred miles they had traversed, and done so at great speed. But their lives had depended on it, and even now Kareste hastened. She sought the cover of the mountain, for there they could rest unobserved in the home of the man who lived there, and need not try to hide in the wild lands where sharp eyes from above might see them.

"Do you think this stranger that we go to will teach us?" Ferla asked.

"We have no guarantee that he'll even put a roof over our heads." Faran looked up at the mountain and frowned. "We know nothing of the man, or how he'll react to us. But if he was a friend of Aranloth, and

Aranloth intended us to go there, then I believe he will help us."

The land they traveled was strangely flat, given the great dome of a mountain that rose up out of it. But it was fertile, and looked to Faran like the creek flats he had known in Dromdruin. The soil was dark and silty, as though floods had deposited it here over many years. But there was no river in sight, nor even a stream.

He thought of the old stories as he walked. Legends sprang up from this place like the grass did from the rich soil. Thousands of stories had their origin here, and then he remembered that the great river of Alithoras, the Careth Nien, ran close by.

Close by was relative. He could not see it, and it was hard to imagine that a river he could not even see could reach the land where he now stood when it flooded. Yet the soil beneath his feet told him it was so.

It was because he was looking downward that he saw the first sword. Mostly, grass grew tall where they went, but here and there were bare patches caused by animal trails, or where wild cattle had grazed it low or made wallows in dust or mud.

It was a rusted thing, barely recognizable for what it was. He knelt down and touched it, and it crumbled at the brush of his fingers.

He saw more as he went. It seemed at one point that the earth itself was made of weapons. Swords he saw, and helms and armor. There were gauntlets too, and belt buckles, harness trappings and all manner of metal objects. Some seemed new enough, and he guessed these were made of elven steel which was said not to tarnish through the long years. But most were nearly returned to the soil like the ore they came from in their forging eons ago.

It was not weapons alone that he saw, and Ferla walked close to him now, her eyes hard and her face pale. There were bones too, long and white where the earth had revealed them to the bleaching sun. Or smooth and domed where there were skulls. And some were not human.

Faran saw many strange things. There were the skulls of elugs, which the old tales sometimes called goblins. They were nearly human, but not quite. There were human skulls too, and he guessed that his forefathers had fought here, some surviving but many dying. This was a graveyard for his people.

But there were Halathrin also. These he learned to recognize by the better-preserved swords that often lay nearby, or by the untarnished helms that sat loosely on gleaming skulls. There were other bones too.

Some were of beasts, massive in size, horned or tusked. Others had the elongated teeth of elù-draks. Some were long and sinuous like snakes, only the size of houses. Were they dragons? He was not sure, but all manner of strange remains he saw, and he was sure that many of them had been lost to history, and the names of them forgotten. Yet legend did say that many creatures of the Shadowed Lord remained in hiding, and he wondered what the king might draw to him with the Morleth Stone.

Kareste fell back to join them, and her face was even more somber than it had been.

"Touch nothing," she warned.

"Why not?" Ferla asked, but Faran knew that was out of curiosity alone. She had been careful where she walked, and he knew she had no intention at all of touching anything.

"This is rumor only," Kareste said. "But there are those who hold the old battlegrounds such as this are haunted. There is elven armor and swords here, not to mention jewels, lying on the earth for any to claim. And such things are priceless. But the stories are all in agreement. Over the years, there have been those who sought plunder, but taking up such objects they became cursed and died horrible deaths within a day. So it is claimed, and there may be truth to it. Magic and sorcery were unleashed in places like this, and even now I feel powers stir beneath my boots."

It was a disturbing thought, and Faran now fancied that he could feel those same forces. Foolishness, of course. He had no real skill in magic, at least compared to Kareste, but he knew that magic, once invoked, had a life of its own.

He felt uncomfortable, and changed the subject. "This man that we go to is a great swordsman, but what will he teach us? Was he once a knight? Will our training be the same as it was?"

Kareste shook her head. "He's not a knight, nor even from this region of Alithoras. What he will teach you, and how, will be far different from the Way of the Sword that the knights know."

Ferla came closer. "That's the whole point, isn't it? To learn how to fight differently from the knights, so that we have an advantage over them?"

Kareste gave her an appraising glance. "That was Aranloth's thinking. He has long trained the knights, and trained them a certain way. And when he was not training them, others who had been trained by him taught in his stead. What you will learn now, hopefully, will be something different. Something the knights aren't used to. It will be a small advantage only, for they are highly skilled. But it will still be an advantage."

Faran knew they would need every advantage they could get. Lindercroft and the king must pay for the crimes they had committed, and now the blood of Aranloth himself demanded it.

4. A Strange Rider

The great mountain drew closer still, and the land about the travelers changed as they walked onward.

Beneath their boots, there were now fewer signs of the battles that had ravished this place in antiquity. There were still artefacts sticking up from the soil where erosion had done its work, and bones too. But fewer of each.

By the time they began to climb upward, traversing the lower rise of the mountain itself, all signs of battle disappeared. The soil changed from silty river deposits into a rich red color, and the grass grew less tall, being of a different variety.

There was a path too, and Kareste led them to it and they followed its steep climb as it zigzagged up the mountain. It was level and smooth, and covered in short grass.

"The elves made this," Kareste said. "The top of the mountain was a lookout for them, and even at times the Halathrin generals directed battles from its plateau."

Faran wondered about that. The battles seemed to have been fought too far away from the mountain top for a general to communicate with an army, but who knew what magic the ancients employed, especially the elves. Legend said they could speak mind to mind. That, or something like it, might account for the problems of distance.

The path, even though it was made so long ago, remained perfectly smooth. There was a camber in the middle that gently sloped to each side. This would shed water in times of heavy rain and help accessibility up or down the mountain even in bad weather. The higher side was lined by stones, and this would divert or slow water that ran off the mountain, while the lower side had no such barrier and allowed easy drainage of rain that fell on the path itself.

It was a steep climb, but already the view was opening up. Sometimes they faced the top of the mountain, but the route wound and turned as it found the best way, and often they faced back toward the lower lands that they had come from.

They kept a close watch as evening fell. It fell quickly too, for they were on the east side of the mountain. Yet there was no sign of any pursuit. If they had been lucky, then their trail away from the valley was undetected. No matter how well they hid it some trail would remain to follow, if the pursuer had sufficient skill. But for that, they would have to know where to start looking, and the boat had helped enormously there.

Luck had played a role too. Rain had fallen on the night of their escape, and that may have obliterated their trail completely. Lindercroft would be searching, but without knowing even the direction his quarry had taken then the area to be searched was massive.

It seemed that all had gone well for them, but Kareste still allowed no fires for fear of giving away their position. Especially, there would be no fire tonight on the side of the mountain. That would stand out for many miles.

They set up camp, eating yet another cold meal. Faran was tired of them, but better cold food than cold steel in his belly. Or the dark sorcery of Lindercroft.

Kareste seemed to read his thoughts. "One more night," she said. "Tomorrow we'll strike for the top of the mountain, and hopefully reach it by dusk. Then, with luck, we'll enjoy a warm fire and a place of shelter to rest unseen."

It was too early to sleep when they were done eating, and by the pale light of stars Faran and Ferla drew their swords and sharpened the blades. It had become a habit lately. It was a grim task, and they took it as a reminder that one day their blades would be used. Each slow stroke of the whetstones was like a step forward in their journey. Today, they fled; but one day they would attack and bring down vengeance upon murderers. And the king was one of them.

Faran grimaced as he ran the stone down the blade. Who was he to bring justice to a Kingshield Knight, still less a king? Yet he knew that he would. Or would die trying.

He saw the same determination in the dark gaze of Ferla. They had not really spoken about it, but they had not needed to. They understood each other, and they both felt the same way and knew it. The deed would be done, or at least attempted. If they did not try, then who would?

The blades did not really seem to need sharpening. There was something in the magic of their making that kept the edges keen, no matter what sparring was done with them. They never chipped or even seemed to blunt.

"Hsst!" Kareste suddenly exclaimed, and she stood up and looked out into the great ocean of dark beneath the mountain.

"What is it?" Ferla asked.

"Something. Nothing. A thing of the past, maybe," Kareste answered mysteriously.

It made no sense to Faran, but following her gaze he saw strange lights at play far below. At first he thought they had been found, and a column of soldiers marched toward them. But then more and more lights showed, dim and shadowy, and some came toward the mountain while others went away from it.

"What *is* it?" Ferla asked.

Faran's skin went cold, and he felt a chill creep up the back of his neck. He remembered an old folktale about dead soldiers from both sides of a conflict fighting their last battle for eternity, their shades contending with one another by light of star and moon to be banished by sunlight at dawn. Yet each night they rose again from their unmarked graves…

Kareste looked at him, and she grinned. "They mean us no harm. Especially you two who are their descendants."

Faran glanced at Ferla, and he saw understanding in her eyes as well. A long time they watched the phantom battles, too far away to see much and glad of the fact. But at length tiredness took them, and they lay down and slept. But Kareste did not. She kept watch for enemies, and long into the night she stood watching. And guarding.

Even as Faran fell asleep, he was reminded of how alike she was to Aranloth. Steadfast and resolute. Tireless in her defense of them. Would she die for her nobility as well, just as Aranloth had? Would she sacrifice herself as the old man had done?

He wished no one to die for him. But he and Ferla could not survive by themselves. Not yet. So they must train harder and learn faster. The sooner they could put themselves in a position where they were a threat to their enemies, the sooner they could transform from hunted into hunter. Then they could return to Faladir and attempt what must be done, and Kareste would be free to leave them to their destiny and follow hers instead.

It rained again overnight, though it was a light shower only, and Faran slept through it. When he woke just before dawn, the lights on the fields below were gone, and he found the others awake before him.

They broke camp quickly, barely taking the time to eat yet one more cold meal of their dwindling reserves, then moved off and climbed the great mountain again.

The mountain was deceptive. It seemed so smooth and rounded from the distant vantage of the plains, but once upon it there were hidden folds and slopes, turning and twisting their way to the top. The path followed them, often taking them through areas of concealment and small valleys. In some of these there were trees, again mostly not visible from a distance.

Kareste led the way, and she hastened even though it was uphill. She had no desire to spend another night in the open, but even she slowed at times to look about her.

At one point she came to a stop and looked around. They were in one of those small valleys, and this one was thickly grown with trees. They were pines, and the needle-like leaves of last year lay thick and brown on the valley floor. But where they had reached now, the trees had grown greater than any Faran had seen before. He saw the wonder in Ferla's eyes, and for the first time in a long while a grin on Kareste's face.

"I have heard tell of this," Kareste said. "These trees grow in a few places in Alithoras, a remnant Aranloth claimed of a once great forest that covered all the land, but I had not known there were any here."

Faran felt the awe of the place. These trees were massive. The bases of some were as big as a house, and the trunks rose, and rose higher, towering into the sky far above until it seemed their very tops were lost in the clouds.

But the trees were not just massive. They were *old*. He felt that, and he felt magic deep in the soil. It was the natural magic of the earth, primal and powerful. It was no wonder that lòhrens were said to favor places such as this. The magic was strong beneath the earth, and the trees brought it forth into the air. It was a place of peace and tranquility, and legend said that when lòhrens grew weary of life they came to places such as this to live out their last years before dying. He believed it.

"These trees stood during the elù-haraken," Kareste said. "They bore witness to terrible battles and awesome magics. And perhaps they will again."

It was not clear exactly what she meant by her last words, but she began again up the trail and Faran and Ferla followed.

The day wore on. They passed through several such valleys as the previous, where the mighty pines grew, but more often they traversed a steady slope, green grass to either side. As they came closer to the summit though, there were no more trees and the grass was shorter, receiving less warmth from the sun to grow.

But these fields were often full of flowers, some tall and bright yellow, while others were small and white-blossomed, creeping through the grass on twining stems.

Most of the plants Faran saw here were foreign to him, and he had no names for them. But he was beginning to like it. The mountain had a feel to it that was different to anywhere else he had ever been.

"What is the name of the man who lives here?" Ferla asked.

"Asana," Kareste replied.

Faran frowned at that. The name, like the mountain, was different from anything he was used to.

"That's not a Camar name," he said.

"Indeed not. Asana was born among the Cheng, and their lands are far, far to the north and west of us."

The Cheng, or at least the name, was familiar to Faran. They were popular in stories, and their fighting skill was legendary. But he had no more chance to talk to Kareste, for they had neared the summit of the mountain.

It was late in the afternoon, and shadows lay over everything, for the setting sun was blocked by the mountain itself. Yet the trail went ahead, and it crested on the plateau just above.

But they paused, for they saw a strange man there. Fierce he looked, and wild. Not least because he sat mounted upon a strange looking horse. No, Faran realized. Not a horse, but a mule, and that was something he had never seen before.

"Welcome to Nuril Faranar," the man said, adjusting the position of a wicked-looking axe that hung from a belt loop.

5. Asana

The travelers paused and took in this new figure. There was a sense of menace to him. He was wild as the mountain itself, and seemed unpredictable and dangerous. But he made no move against them.

"Is that Asana?" whispered Faran.

"Perhaps," Kareste answered. "But I think not."

The lòhren walked ahead, but Faran noticed that she held her staff loosely in her hand, yet still ready for action.

"May we come to the top?" Kareste called.

The strange figure on the mule gave no answer. Instead, he nudged it backward from the crest and disappeared.

Kareste did not hesitate, and strode upward. Faran and Ferla followed. In just a few moments they reached the plateau. It was not quite level atop the mountain, but it was close to it. And it was bigger than Faran would have believed if he had not seen it.

There was room for a farm here, if only a small one. There were acres of grassland, and some trees. But these were fruit trees rather than anything wild. There were gardens also, both vegetable and ornamental, and everything was neat as could be. Even the vegetable rows were laid out with a precision that he had never seen before, arrow straight and weed free.

He took in the view too. It was vast, stretching out in all directions, though the light was fading and he could not see some things clearly. But to the south, he saw the winding gleam of the Careth Nien, and to the south and west was the smudge on the horizon of a mighty forest that marched out of view toward the westering sun. That, he knew, was Halathar, the forest home of the immortal elves.

He took all that in at a glance, but his gaze was swiftly drawn to the stranger. The wild man had dismounted from the mule, and he walked toward them.

"Hey!" he said. "Did you see the ghosts fight last night? It was a good show! I nearly went down among them."

"We did," Kareste said, and she leant upon her staff as she spoke just like Aranloth used to. Faran felt tears swell in his eyes and fought them back.

"Does that happen every night?" Kareste continued.

"Hardly," the wild man said. "It's hard to predict. Sometimes it's every night in the week. Other times a month might pass. The dead have no sense of time, I guess. I envy them though."

"How so?"

The strange man looked at Kareste as though she were a simpleton.

"What's better than a good fight? A man knows he's alive when the blades flash in the air. Even the dead must feel that."

Kareste grinned at him, but Faran was not so sure she agreed. Maybe she just liked him for all his oddness. Or maybe she was just being careful.

"My name is—"

"I know who you are," the wild man interrupted, scratching his armpit. "You're Kareste, a lòhren. And you bring with you Ferla and Faran. Two who seek training in the arts of the Cheng."

Kareste showed no surprise, and Faran admired her for that. It was not possible that this man knew who they were or what they wanted. Yet he did.

"And would you be Asana, the swordsman?"

The strange man laughed at that, and he slapped his thighs and shook his axe in the air by turns, dancing a little jig.

Faran watched him, and wondered if he were sane.

"That's a fine jest!" the man exclaimed at length. "At least I think so. Asana might not, though. I fear he wouldn't see the funny side of it. He rarely does."

The man slipped the axe back in its loop and went back for his mule. However strange he seemed, he was an athlete. He mounted the mule in one smooth motion and Faran got the feeling that he could wield that axe of his to deadly effect.

"I'm Kubodin," he said, looking down at them with a grin. "I'll take you to the master. He sent me to greet you, but I think you could have found the way by yourselves. But he's like that. He's one for politeness, he is."

He nudged the mule forward, and they fell in beside him. The day was dying around them, but there was still light enough to see.

Faran saw no sign of a house or cottage. None at all. Yet there were gardens everywhere of all sorts, and paths through them. Nor were the gardens just for beauty or food. As night settled around them, scents filled the air from various flowers, or arose from the leaves of bushes on the edges of the path that they brushed as they passed. Or even of small plants that they trod underfoot.

They reached the heart of the plateau, and the stars kindled to life in the dark sky above as the glow of the setting sun faded in the west. Here, there was a circle of trees.

They were pines, but not the massive variety that grew in the valleys on the mountain slopes. These were just like them, and old they seemed, yet they grew upward only the span of three men.

Kubodin dismounted, and he led them forward on foot from here.

The path was well trodden, though like everything else it was extraordinarily neat. Shrouded by some bushes was a small corral where Kubodin led the mule and released him. The bushes were positioned so as to allow the sun into the enclosure during winter but to offer shade in summer. There was also a small area, roofed and walled on three sides, for shelter during bad weather.

Kubodin lifted some wooden rails in place to close the corral.

"I'll take you to the master now."

Faran looked around, and he felt uneasy. There was nothing else here. But Kubodin merely grinned at him, and beckoned everyone to follow.

He did not go far. There was a small outcrop of rock close by, thrust up from the mountain. Here Kubodin looked back at them, and he offered something that might have been a bow, but it looked ill-practiced.

"Welcome to our humble house." Then he fiddled with something shoulder high on the stone outcrop. It sat on some sort of rugged shelf, and then light sprang up from a lantern.

Even so, the opening was still hard to see. But there was one there, wide and tall enough for a man to pass through. This Kubodin proved, taking the lantern with him and disappearing inside.

Kareste merely shrugged and followed after. Faran and Ferla looked at each other, and he could see that she was not overly pleased. No doubt she hoped for better shelter than a cave, but beggars could not be choosers as the saying went.

He followed her inside, and was immediately surprised. This was no cave, but a tunnel. The walls were perfectly smooth, and it was now wide enough for a small group of people to walk through side by side. The floor was not of natural stone. It was laid with oven-baked tiles, and there were mosaics of different colors and designs. Some were geometric patterns, but often there were images of trees, flowers, birds and beasts. Some were of types that Faran had never seen before.

Kubodin scratched himself and grinned. He seemed pleased at their surprise.

"The Halathrin made this," he said, gesturing around himself. "My master says that Halath himself walked here, and it may be true. But the elves are long gone now, and they don't leave their forest."

The light of the lantern danced around as he moved, and Kareste tapped the tip of her staff against the tiles and a bright light sprang from its tip.

Kubodin eyed her a moment. "Hey! That's good magic," he said. "A nice trick. Maybe you'll teach me someday?"

"If you wish. But not everyone has the talent, or the willpower for the long years of training."

Kubodin shrugged. "You sound just like my master. But he awaits below, so let's go. He'll be mad if I don't bring you down quickly."

They followed him down the tunnel. There were no side branches. At least none that Faran could see. But it would not be hard to conceal doors here. The walls were often decorated too, as well as the ceiling. There were numerous places that would hide any doorway. But he did not think this place had been built with a special eye for defense. The long tunnel itself offered a place where a few men, or elves, could defend well for a long time, and withdraw slowly if they were pressed back.

Faran walked easily. Despite being underground, this place was nothing like the tombs of the Letharn, and there was nothing dangerous down here. Except, perhaps, the greatest swordsman of the age. That was dangerous enough, but if Aranloth had wished to come here, then this man would likely be friendly.

There were colored lamps set in shelves from time to time, and Kubodin lit these as they passed. Soon the whole tunnel glowed, and the designs all about them came to life in the wavering light.

Kareste lowered her staff, and the light at its tip went out. Kubodin saw that and smiled to himself, but he said nothing. It seemed to Faran that the man only lit the lamps to show that magic was not needed, but he might have been imagining that.

At length, the tunnel came to an end. It opened into a central room, round in shape. It was large, perhaps forty yards or more across, yet there were no pillars to hold up the roof. And if the tunnel was well decorated, this room was more so. The floor tiles gleamed in the light, for there were many lamps set in niches within the wall.

The walls themselves were covered in carvings, reaching high into the hidden ceiling above. On the floor were rugs, spaced neatly apart, and there were several tables and chairs, as well as multiple fireplaces set into the walls, yet only one contained a fire at present.

"Hey! Master, you can stop combing your hair now."

It was only when Kubodin spoke that Faran realized a figure sat on one of those chairs. The chair was large, almost like a throne, and the figure had been perfectly still.

"I was not combing my hair, Kubodin."

"What then? Were you trimming your eyebrows again?"

"Neither was I doing that." The figure stood in a smooth motion, and came toward them.

Faran studied him, and felt a chill. He had only seen a conjured image of Brand rather than the real thing, but this man before him had the same deadly grace. He made no hostile move, yet the potential for death hovered all around him. But just like Brand, for all the hardness of his eyes there was a kindliness there also.

The strange man came closer, all subtle grace and hidden death. He did not wear boots, but rather delicate shoes of white cloth, though they must still have a leather sole. His long tunic was also white, and of a fabric that Faran had never seen before. It seemed soft and luxurious beyond his imaginings. A sword hung from his waist, and the man wore it as naturally as another might don a cloak in cold weather.

"Welcome to Danath Elbar," the man greeted them, "where once the high lords of the elves met with their king and decided the fate of nations."

6. You are Observant

Kareste stepped forward. "My name is—"

"I know who you are," the stranger said quietly. "You are Kareste, a lòhren, and friend of Aranloth, who is also my friend. And your companions are Ferla and Faran."

He bowed then to Kareste, and gazed at Ferla intently for a moment before he bowed to her also. Then lastly he bowed to Faran.

"How is it that you know us?" Kareste asked.

"I know some things, but many others remain hidden. But first, allow me to introduce myself. I am Asana. For the moment, I dwell here at the pleasure of the elves. But my name at least you already know, for Aranloth sent you to me."

Kareste held the man's gaze. "You have the Sight, do you not?"

Asana sighed. "I am blessed with visions from time to time." He looked suddenly sad as he spoke. "Or cursed with them, if you prefer. Sometimes I do."

He paused then, and glanced at them all thoughtfully.

"To make the matter clear to you, I know who you are, and who you flee and why. I also know why Aranloth sent you to me."

Kareste nodded slowly. "Will you do it then? Will you shelter us and teach these two Cheng Fah, the Way of the Warrior? Even if it endangers you, as you know it will?"

Asana's face showed little emotion, but the sadness in his eyes deepened.

"You are hasty folk, at least compared to the Cheng. I find that ... refreshing. So I will give you a direct answer."

His gaze fell again to Ferla and then Faran. "I will teach as best I can, for I owe Aranloth. Even if I did not, I would still help you, for your quest is noble and it serves the land. The evil in Faladir will not stay there. It will grow and spread. It will conquer nation after nation, unless it is stopped. And therefore I will play my role in the events to come."

Asana turned to Kubodin. "You have done well, as always. Are their rooms prepared also?"

The other man pulled his pants a little higher, which the axe seemed to be weighing down, and tightened his belt. He did not seem to care that he did this in company.

"I'm no butler. But hey, I did what you asked. The rooms are ready. I'm sure our guests will be as comfortable as pigs in mud on their birthday."

Asana did not seem to notice the man's actions or his tone of voice. For that matter, Faran was becoming adjusted to them quickly himself, nor did he think any offence was intended. The man just had a direct way of speaking.

"Yes," Asana agreed. "You are no butler."

Faran detected the slightest note of amusement in the man's voice.

Asana bowed again. "Kubodin will take you to your rooms, and he will provide you with food also. Though I fear you will miss eating meat while you stay here. We eat only vegetables, but of those we have many varieties." He glanced at his servant, and the smile flickered over his face again briefly. "Kubodin is a better cook than he is a butler."

"I'm no servant," Kubodin said. "And the master knows it. I'm a warrior, even if I don't have a pretty sword like his."

"My sword is not pretty," Asana answered. "It is a tool of death, and death follows me." He faced toward

Kareste. "May you all sleep well. In the morning, I will begin to train your charges, but for now I feel the need to meditate."

That faint smile on his face was gone, and he seemed sad again, or resigned to something he did not like.

Kubodin shuffled off, somehow ungainly and graceful at the same time, and they followed him. There were corridors that led away from this central chamber, and he moved to the closet one on the left.

The corridor was not long. Kubodin lit another lantern within it, but soon they came to a doorway. This was made of timber, and Faran did not think it was the original. It was plain, unlike the stonework, and the Halathrin were renowned for their woodwork.

Beyond was a large chamber. Again, the floor was marvelously decorated, and if the ceiling was lower than in the main room it was still high. Frescoes decorated it, depicting forests and hunts and swift streams racing amid dark tracts of pines.

It was luxury such as Faran had never seen but had heard tell of in stories. There was a long table also, for meals, and various padded chairs.

Kubodin pointed to the back of the chamber where there were yet more doors.

"Over there you will find several bedrooms. Pick and choose them as they seem best to you. This," he said, gesturing around him, "is a communal living area for you all."

Faran could not believe it. He had loved the cottage in the valley, but this was a palace by comparison.

"Thank you, Kubodin," Kareste said. "You and your master are most hospitable."

Kubodin seemed uncomfortable at that, but before he could give any answer Ferla asked him a question.

"Why is Asana so sad? He tries to hide it, but I can see it in his eyes."

Kubodin glanced at her sharply. "You are observant, you are. Yes. Very. I have noticed the same thing lately, but I don't know why. He won't tell me what's wrong."

For all the rough ways of this man, Faran suddenly saw how much he cared for his friend.

"Time will reveal it, one way or the other," he continued. "I'll bring you some food shortly."

He left then, sauntering out in his strange walk, and adjusting the axe at his side once more. Why he had not put it down earlier, Faran did not know. But he unbelted his own sword and placed it in a corner of the room. Ferla did likewise, and they removed their armor as well. For the first time in days, Faran felt safe.

They sat down around the table and talked quietly. At least Faran and Ferla did. Kareste seemed thoughtful, though what she was trying to puzzle out Faran could not tell.

"At least we know that Asana will teach us," Ferla said. "I'd feared that he would not."

Kareste stirred. "You should know that the Cheng rarely teach their skills to outsiders, still less one of Asana's standing. You are more privileged than you know."

"Tell us about the Cheng," Faran asked. "Asana does look foreign, but not nearly so much as Kubodin."

Kareste grinned. "I *like* Kubodin. What you see is what you get. Asana, though I trust him because Aranloth did, well, I just cannot quite figure him out. His mind is closed to me, but he is only half Cheng according to what Aranloth told me. His father was of the Duthenor, but his mother was a Cheng lady."

"Strange that you should say that," Faran said. "When I first saw him, he reminded me of Brand."

Kareste did not answer that. Instead, she told them more of the Cheng.

"They once had a vast empire," she said. "It was a long time after the fall of the Letharn, but still ancient history to us."

Faran listened carefully. This might better help him to understand Asana, and that was important. If the man was going to teach him swordsmanship, Faran wanted to be a good student. He wanted to learn. He *needed* to learn, and insight into his teacher was key to that.

Kareste continued. "They were a mighty nation, and their skills and arts were advanced. But they were also a warrior people, so much so that even their name itself, Cheng, is also their word for warrior."

She sat back in her chair, thoughtful. "Even Aranloth never knew their full history. And they were a long way away even from the borders of the old Letharn empire. But they traded with the Duthenor and Camar, even before those tribes came east to settle the coastal tracts of Alithoras."

It occurred to Faran that she spoke of the Duthenor and Camar tribes from the outside, as though she was not one of them. What nationality was she, then? There was a look about her too that was different, if even just slightly, from the people he had known all his life.

"It was inevitable with the trade," she went on, "that not only goods passed from hand to hand but ideas passed from mind to mind. That included military strategies and the arts of the warrior, for traders always brought bodyguards with them. So some of what you have already learned derives from the Cheng, changed by the years and developed to suit Camar swords and armor, which are somewhat different from the Cheng."

She looked at them both earnestly. "But what you will learn now are those same arts, refined by the Cheng over the years, and made different by that passage of time as the descendants of two families change through the generations. This will give you a perspective, and skills, none of the knights possess, not to mention you will learn it from perhaps the greatest swordsman alive. Heed him well, for his kind is rarer than snow on midsummer's day."

Ferla nodded. "I can tell just by the way he moves how dangerous he is. Honestly, I'm excited to learn from him."

Faran thought the same. This was not where he wanted to be, or what he wanted to be doing, but fate had served it up to him, and he would make the most of it.

They talked a little more, and not long after Kubodin returned.

"Food!" he said. "You may find it different from what you're used to, but it'll fill your belly."

Saying that, he placed two large platters down on the table.

"More to come!" he told them, "But don't wait. Cold food tastes like a badger's armpit!"

Faran had no idea about that, but he had eaten cold rations for too long, and the sight of steaming food was delicious to him.

There was no meat, which was a disappointment, but there was a large array of vegetables and grains. Most came in startling sauces that tasted like nothing Faran had ever eaten before, but he liked some of them very much.

They had not finished when Kubodin returned. He carried more platters, and on each were delicate bowls of fine porcelain. Within these were yet more strange foods, and Faran wanted to try them all.

They did not talk much while they ate, for they were tired from their hasty journey, and the warm food, and so much of it too, that they grew sleepy.

Soon they explored the rooms at the far end of the chamber, and selected their bedrooms. There was little in these, but there were comfortable beds and Faran put his head down and fell asleep swiftly. Tomorrow was a new day, and a new stage in his life. He wanted to be ready for whatever it would bring.

7. A Wise Man is Prepared

Asana sat in the High Seat in the central chamber where he had met the travelers, and thought.

The chair was one of the few original items left in these underground halls. Halath himself might have sat in this same chair, probably in this same spot, and felt the burdens of the world.

Asana sighed. Just as he did. Kubodin sat opposite him, on the ground. Chairs were for the nobility the little man always claimed, and he would not use one even though there were several others in the room, if smaller. He also said that sitting in a soft chair made one's backside soft, which in turn caused a soft brain, but that was Kubodin for you.

The evening had passed quietly, and it was now deep into the night. His guests had eaten well, and now slept. He wished he could do the same, but of late sleep came with difficulty. Not so with Kubodin. The man could sleep on any surface, anywhere, day or night. Nothing seemed to trouble him, and Asana envied that.

Perhaps it was his own fault. He overthought things. This was a trait that Kubodin did not have, though the little man surprised the unobservant. For all his peasant ways, he had one of the sharpest minds Asana had ever encountered. He just chose not to put it on display.

Kubodin stirred from his position on the floor. He looked upward.

"Why so sad, master?"

Asana was surprised. Of course, he did not show that. A gentleman retained balance at all times, neither showing surprise or anticipation.

Kubodin did have the habit of asking questions like that when least expected. It was his way of trying to get an unfiltered answer, and to slip past Asana's guard.

It was true though, and he had no wish to lie to his friend. Yet still, he would not burden him with foreknowledge of tragedy.

He forced a smile. "Who says that I am sad?"

"I do. I've seen it these last few days. Even the girl sees it, and she doesn't know you."

"She is observant, that one. But she will need to be."

Kubodin ignored that. He knew it was an attempt to change the subject.

"You didn't answer my question."

"I am not sad. Nor am I happy. I seek the Path of Nature, which is simply to exist peacefully, to accept fate with equilibrium and to shun the desires of humanity which inevitably lead to misfortune."

"Pah! You and your Path. It's no way for a man to live. Breathe deep instead, feel the heat of a fire or the cold blast of a winter wind. Feel the warmth of a woman in your bed, and hone your hatred of enemies until it becomes cold steel. That's how to live!"

"It is one way to live."

Kubodin shook his head. "Still, you ignore my question."

The night was growing old, and Asana did not want to talk of this. Yet he did still want to talk, and he was curious about their guests. Each, in their way, was intriguing.

"Tell me of the newcomers. What do you think of them? Start with the lòhren."

Kubodin frowned, no doubt annoyed at his question being put off again, yet his expression turned thoughtful at the task set him.

"She isn't like Aranloth. Not a bit. Except where it counts. Her loyalty is strong, and she wouldn't abandon her charges though all the forces of hell descended on her in fire and fury."

Asana considered that. Kubodin was the shrewdest judge of character that he knew, and the little man's judgement matched his own.

"I agree. But speaking of Aranloth, where is he? I expected him to arrive with the others."

Kubodin did not seem concerned. "It's probably just as well. More guests are more work, and I have enough of that already."

"Nevertheless, I will ask in the morning. His absence disturbs me." Asana thought some more. "Now, tell me what you think of the girl Ferla. Apart from the fact that she is observant."

Kubodin did not answer straight away, and Asana liked that. Someone who always had answers ready to hand had not pondered deeply and their responses were suspect.

"She may be fit for the task fate has set her. Many would break, but she may survive it. Maybe. I hope so. There is certainly no lack of willpower, and there is a quiet spark in her eyes. I like that."

"Did you notice how she looked at Faran? There are strong feelings there."

Kubodin grinned. "He has them too. They're good for each other, those two. The loyalty between them is strong as iron."

Asana wondered if there was more than loyalty and friendship between them. But whatever they had, it would be tested to the limit.

"What of the young man?"

"He is the hardest of all to judge. An anger burns in him, and that's good. A man needs a fire in his belly if he wants to achieve anything."

"But?" Asana asked.

"He's hasty, I think. He hasn't learned patience yet. From what you told me, he has reason enough for anger, but it could be his undoing. In my village, there's a saying. *Let the heart grow cold with anger. Meanwhile, forge a knife in the hottest coals, and when it is ready, sharpen it for three winters*."

Asana did not grin. He found Kubodin's sayings inscrutable sometimes, but that one was clear enough.

"I agree. Yet he has the markings of greatness to him. If he lives long enough to come into his own."

"And what is his destiny? You have not told me that."

Asana wished he knew for certain, but at the moment he only guessed.

"I am not sure. Sometimes my visions are clear. Other times, they are not. With him, it is as though the path he walks goes into mist. I have caught only glimpses."

Kubodin grunted. His manners were certainly lacking, but not his mind.

"What of the enemy?" the little man asked. "They're the second half of the story, but I know little of them."

It was a good question, and Asana considered his answer. His friend wanted to calculate the chances of victory his guests had, which was wise. But it was also futile, for destiny was moving among them, and strange things could happen.

"The enemy are the Kingshield Knights, as you know. And the king, also one of their order, who leads them."

Kubodin grew impatient. "Yes, I know that. It's what you told me before. But *why* are they doing this? From what I hear, they're supposed to be a force of good in the world."

"I was getting to that," Asana said gently. "Patience."

Kubodin gave him a sour look. The man was expert at that. He had more ranges of expression for sourness than most people could find for the entire range of human emotion.

"Have your people heard of Morleth Stones?" Asana asked.

"Oh, that's bad. Very bad magic. The worst of magics." The little man even shivered, as though just thinking of it somehow cast a shadow over him. "But I see now what has happened. I know the origin of the knights. Who hasn't heard that tale? Even deep in the hills," he muttered sarcastically. "The knights have used the stone and been subverted to its will."

Asana had not thought of it like that before. His friend spoke as though the stone were alive. What else had a will, but the living? Yet it might be so.

"So my vision showed me. The knights grow strong, and they were fine warriors before that."

Kubodin hugged his knees up to his chest. "Oh, this is even worse than I thought. Our guests are hunted by a great evil, and one that'll grow stronger."

"Yes," Asana agreed. "Are they up to it?"

"Hey! Why ask me? I don't see the visions you do."

"I ask you because you are a shrewd judge of character."

"Let me think," Kubodin said. "I don't know why you care anyway. You and your kind are always trying to plan ahead. It's no way to live. If a poisonous snake crawls before your feet, cut off its head. If it bites and kills you instead, then you die. Why worry about either until it happens? But hey, what do I know?"

Asana now knew what his friend's answer was. He just did not want to say it. He thought to spare him.

"Say what you think, Kubodin."

"As if I always don't. But since you ask, I'll say this. For all their courage, and they must have a lot to have survived this long, they cannot win. But who cares? It's the fight that counts. And this will be a good one."

Asana gave the slightest of nods. That was also his assessment. They could not really hope to prevail against what came against them, but that was inevitable. Life itself was a battle of survival from cradle to the grave, and no one won that battle for long. It was the way of nature, and the end did not matter. It was what one did while alive that counted, and death and defeat did not change that. He had a feeling his guests, each of them in turn, would account for themselves well. As he would try to do.

"You will help me to help them, despite their chances?"

Kubodin grinned wickedly. "Of course! They're my sort of people, and they'll poke the enemy in the eye a few times. I like that!"

"Very well, then. First thing in the morning, I want you to scout around below the mountain. See if you find anything of note."

"You think the enemy may have tracked them here?"

Asana's vision had not been clear on this. He knew the enemy would find them. But he was not sure when, and it was best that way.

"I do not think so. But the wise man is prepared."

Kubodin rose to his feet in one smooth motion. For all that he looked a shabby layabout, he was strong and lithe.

"Don't start with the wise man stuff again." He adjusted his axe in its belt loop. "I don't think I'll find anything. That lòhren isn't the type to bring trouble to others. If she were followed, she wouldn't have come here. But you do think the enemy will find them, sooner or later, yes?"

"Sooner or later," Asana agreed.

Kubodin looked at him intently, as though he had just discerned something, then he turned on his heels and left.

It was past time to sleep. Well past it. But Asana sat in the High Chair and continued to think.

8. First Training

Early the next day, Faran and Ferla donned their armor. They had no idea what to expect of their new teacher, but first impressions counted and they wanted to be seen to be keen.

In truth, they *were* keen. This was a chance to learn from one of the greatest swordsmen alive. They had no doubt that he was better than the knights. All that remained was to learn as much from him as they could, and hope that they mastered enough of it so they could match the knights when the time came.

So it was that they retraced their steps from last night, going first to the central chamber where they had met their host. But he was not there, and they moved up the tunnel and out onto the mountaintop.

There was no sign of Kubodin, and Kareste remained below. But Asana was there, and the first rays of the sun were spearing the sky from the east.

"I trust you slept well?" Asana asked, rising from where he sat on the dewy grass.

"Yes, thank you," Ferla answered.

Faran had slept well, but he was not sure about Asana. The man hid it, but he seemed tired as though he had not slept at all, and there was a troubled look to his gaze.

"In my country," Asana told them, "the warrior limbers up at dawn, going through a series of exercises. Their purpose is for health, but a limber and strong body is a prerequisite to fine swordsmanship. Will you join me in this routine?"

It was worded as a question, but Faran sensed that this was a man used to being obeyed. So he nodded, and Ferla did likewise beside him.

"Then let us begin. Follow me as best you can."

He moved ahead of them and faced the rising sun. His sword was not belted at his side, but rather lay on the grass nearby. They placed theirs next to it. Then moving slowly, and breathing deeply, he took them through a series of movements unlike anything Faran had seen before. They were smooth and graceful, yet at the same time pushed the body to its limits in terms of flexibility.

Nor were they easy. Some of the low stances made Faran's legs tremble, and he knew he was far away from executing the movements with anything like the grace of this master. But he would try, and he would get better over time. He saw the value in this, for suppleness rather than brute strength was the hallmark of a good swordsman.

Asana did not teach. In this, he was different from Aranloth who often explained things. But now, if Faran wanted to learn, he must observe closely and mimic. Then, by slow reasoning of his own, work out why a thing was done the way it was and what benefits it would accrue.

When they were finished, Asana took them through it again. Then a third time, this time sometimes watching them and correcting their movements without words but a touch here and there on their limbs.

After the third time, Asana retrieved his sword and belted it.

"Tomorrow, do not wear your armor. There is value in getting used to wearing it at all times, but it restricts your movements in exercises such as this. But you will, of course, wear it when sword training."

He eyed them closely. "Have you yet reached the point where you spar with real swords?"

"We have," Ferla replied.

"Then it is time for me to see what your skill is. You may spar, but be careful."

Faran drew his sword, and it felt good in his hand. But a grin was on Ferla's face, and he knew she was enjoying this. They had not trained since the valley, and they both missed it.

Ferla swung an overhand blow at him, but at the last moment swayed and tilted, bringing the blade in at a sidewise angle.

She nearly hit him with the side of the blade, but he had seen her hips move and knew the change was coming. Just in time, he leaped back. He could not parry because she had caught him out in the wrong position, his arms raised to block the overhand strike that had never come.

He moved quickly, but she had anticipated his response and was upon him with great speed.

Three times he parried her blade, twice deflecting neatly and the third time forced into blocking with sheer force.

Her fourth strike struck him. It was a stab to the belly, and he felt the force of it through his armor although she withheld almost all its power.

They stepped back and started again. This time they circled each other, moving with slow sideways steps and looking for a weakness. Faran found none, but he attacked anyway. He turned from a sidestep into a lunge, and stabbed toward her. Deftly, she deflected his strike and sent a counterblow toward his helmed head.

He was ready for it, and he guided it away then shuffled forward and kicked at her knee. This caught her a glancing blow, and she grunted in surprise but was already out of reach for his follow up sword stroke.

They circled again, carefully assessing every move the other made, looking for a moment when their footing was off balance, or an opening presented itself in their sword guard.

But there was none. Instead, Asana clapped his hands and called for a halt.

He gazed at them impassively, his deep brown eyes revealing nothing of what he thought, but his words did.

"Aranloth trained you well. How long were you with him?"

"Last summer and winter," Ferla told him.

"Remarkable," Asana said softly. "Your skill is far above what it should be for so little time training. I have seen students study for years and not reach your attainment."

Faran knew why, but he said nothing. It was magic that had done it, that ability Aranloth had to lay his mind over theirs and show them what was possible. That, and sparring the conjured images of swordsmen like Brand. How could they have failed to prosper under such tuition?

"Where *is* Aranloth?" Asana asked.

A wave of grief washed over Faran, and it was Ferla who answered.

"He is dead. The enemy killed him while we escaped."

At that Asana raised an eyebrow. It was the most emotion Faran had seen him display.

"Are you sure of this? Aranloth is, well, frankly … he is a hard man to kill."

"As sure as we can be. We escaped through an underground tunnel, and he was supposed to come through after us. But he never did, so he ended up facing the enemy all alone."

Asana frowned. "Did you see his body?"

"No, but there was no way he could be alive."

Asana shrugged. "We shall see. If he is dead, it is a greater loss to the world than you know. But I will not believe it myself. I cannot."

Faran felt the same way. There was no hope, but it *was* true that they had seen no body.

Asana stepped closer. "May I examine your swords? They are not like any blades that I have seen before."

Faran reversed his sword, and handed it over hilt first.

Asana took it carefully, holding it with something close to reverence. Whether he did that for all swords or just this one, Faran was not sure.

"It has a good balance," Asana said, swinging it gently through the air. "The grip is good, the blade lighter than it looks."

"It was forged by the ancient Letharn," Faran told him.

"Well can I believe it. But how did you come by such blades?"

"Aranloth took us to the Tombs of the Letharn," Ferla said. "There are many such blades there, but these he chose just for us."

Asana let out a long and slow breath. "I have heard of such blades. Even as I have heard of the tombs. But I never thought to hold such a weapon. There is magic in the steel, yes?"

"There is," Faran admitted. "But it's no aid against other swordsmen. It's only useful against sorcery."

Asana sighed. "I would give much for a blade such as this. Then again, I would wish no other than the one I carry, that my forefathers carried before me."

He returned the sword to Faran. "Use it well. May it protect you. You will find as I teach you that many of my techniques are designed for a lighter blade. But that is of no matter. The principles of swordsmanship are the same, and there is no such thing as a single and right technique. They all must be adapted to suit the blade you carry, and your natural strengths. Together, we will do just that."

Something occurred to Faran. "You don't seem to wear armor. Will that change things as well?"

Asana nodded approvingly. "A good question. Yes it will. Knowing that you may survive a thrust to the belly or a strike to the head because of chainmail or helm changes how you move. But again, we will work on these differences. I wear no armor, and that is a disadvantage. On the other hand, I have some modicum of skill, and my sword is sharper than yours. It can cut through bone, and armor is less an impediment than you might think to a sword such as mine."

Faran could hardly believe that, yet the quiet little man did not seem at all the type to boast or make false claims.

"Follow me now," Asana said, "and I will show you one of the patterns I know. It will better suit your blades than some others."

He drew his sword, and for the first time Faran got a look at it. It was slightly shorter than his, and certainly narrower and thinner. It was not a blade meant for hacking into armor, but for quick slices and deadly thrusts. How sharp it was, he could not tell. But the steel glimmered wickedly, and Faran did not doubt that it was very, very sharp.

Asana spun and leapt, the blade flickering through the air and his every movement impossible grace.

Faran followed a moment later, trying to copy the move. Ferla did likewise beside him. Asana paused, holding his posture so they could study the angle of his limbs, the position of his body and the placement of his feet. Then he drove forward in another attack, this time a slash at an opponent's neck.

This they followed also, adjusting their positions to try to match the master. And on their training proceeded, following him through the entire pattern. It was a beautiful form, made for lighter swords than their own, but with practice Faran knew they could master it, and also its subtleties. For it contained many movements that he was not sure the exact purpose of, but they seemed to be attacks designed to sever sword hands, nick arteries in the arm and puncture the great blood vessels of the neck, all with the slightest of movements disguised within larger strokes.

"That is enough for today," Asana called. "I will think on your skills, and how to better them."

"Thank you," Ferla said.

Faran offered a bow.

"That is not the end of your training though. A limber body, and skill with weapons is not enough. In my country, a warrior, if he or she is to become the best, must also become a sage. A person of wisdom. For the true warrior knows why they fight, for whom and whether or not it is just. How else can they choose to participate?"

Aranloth had often said much the same thing, and Faran was glad of this turn. He liked the sword lessons, but even better was the strengthening of his mind. He was not, nor would ever be again, just the simple hunter who had roamed Dromdruin's dark forests.

"Follow me," Asana commanded.

He led them through the ring of trees and toward the south side of the plateau. The smudge on the horizon that was Halathar, the forest realm of the immortal elves, was much clearer today. The sky was blue and the air was clear. But up here, at this height, Faran knew that might change quickly. He wondered where Kubodin was, for he had seen no sign of him all morning, but he was sure the little man would show up. Faran was surprised to realize that he liked him.

Asana took them to the edge of the plateau, where there was a steep stretch down a rolling incline. On the precipice, was a little patch of grass. It was neatly cut by some tool, and the ground was flat. No doubt, this was Kubodin's handiwork.

Asana sat, and gestured for Faran and Ferla to join him. They did so, taking up positions to either side and admiring the view.

"The Halathrin are wise," Asana said softly. "They have withdrawn from the world and left troubles behind them. Here, on this mountain, I have done something similar." He paused for a moment, and shifted his glance to Ferla first and then Faran. "Do you agree?"

Ferla answered swiftly. "It may be wise. Certainly, I can imagine that it brings peace. But not forever. Sooner or later the outside world will intrude on the elves even as we have intruded on you."

Asana seemed surprised by that answer, but he gave a sad little grin.

"You may be an intrusion, but you are most welcome." He turned to Faran. "What do you think?"

"I'm a hunter. I love nature and the quiet of the forest. I love being alone. And though I wish it were otherwise, what Ferla says is true. The outside world intrudes. But that does not make it *unwise* to try to find tranquility."

Those sad, brown eyes of Asana gazed out toward the distant forest.

"Two very different answers, and yet the same in their way. Grief is a good teacher of wisdom, is it not?"

Faran nodded, but did not speak.

"When trouble comes to the elves, as you predict it will one day, what should they do? Seek to seclude themselves even deeper into the forest? Or fight for a just cause, even if it kills them?"

It seemed a strange question to Faran. What did this have to do with their training? But at the same time, for all the inscrutability that Asana showed, Faran sensed that the man waited with extreme curiosity for their answer.

"Who can say what is right or wrong?" Ferla answered. "Both courses of action may seem wise. Yet inner conscience will dictate how a people, or a person, will act under such circumstances. And by their actions they will show what they are made of."

Asana did not take his eyes off the horizon. "You are correct."

9. The Hundred

Menendil inserted the spigot in the new ale keg atop the bar. This was a good brew, made by himself as they all were, but it was a pity there were few customers around to enjoy it. And some of those that were there, he did not like.

He turned to his wife. "This is a good batch, love. The best for some while."

Norla did not stop polishing the glass she was working on, and she spared him only the slightest of glances before concentrating fully on the glass again as though it was the most important thing in the world.

"Better than this lot deserve," she muttered. "We should charge more."

She was still unhappy with what he had done. It showed in her every glance. But it was too late now to go back on things.

Perhaps she was right. Perhaps not. But she was wrong about raising the price of ale. That would offset their lower take since customers had nearly stopped coming in, especially at night. But they would find another place to drink, and fast if he did that. Better to keep the customers he did have and wait things out until better times. If they ever came.

He poured a young man a glass of the ale when he came over. The man did not say thanks, and he was slow enough to pass the coins for it over the counter too. Typical. Some people wanted everything for nothing as though the world owed it to them.

He would learn though. The young man went back to sit with his friends. They were a lot like him, only worse. There were thieves among them, of that Menendil was sure. You did not keep a bar without learning to be a good judge of people.

"You'll get us killed. You know that, don't you?"

His wife had come closer without him noticing, and she continued the gist of the conversation they had been having all morning. She was careful that no one could hear them, though.

They rarely argued. The worst thing about this one was that she was right. But what else could he have done?

"Would you really stand by," he answered, "and let evil overrun the city?"

To that, she gave no answer. But his words did not remove her scowl. He had a feeling that nothing would. Not anytime soon.

"Anyway," he went on, carefully looking around the room to make sure no one was watching or could hear. "The Hundred are selected and gathered. The way is prepared if it is needed."

He did not say it was prepared for the seventh knight. Even thinking that was dangerous, and just a few days ago he had heard of an inn burned to the ground by the king's soldiers because a storyteller had told the tale of the prophecy.

The knowledge that he risked death, and the death of his wife and the destruction of all that he held dear was a burden to him. Yet the love of truth and justice must be served also. All the more so if it came at risk, and it was not in him to back away from that, come what may.

There were others who felt like him. Some could not act. They did not know how. But he did. He was a former soldier. An elite soldier. Danger was not new to him, nor planning how to counter it.

And he had planned well.

In the far corner, farthest away from the table of young men, Norgril sat by himself. He was second in command of the Hundred, and he was a man to be trusted. He was skilled too, though a little hotheaded and prone to act first and think later.

The two of them were friends, but they spoke as little as possible now. It was better that way, for by distancing themselves they each gave the other some small measure of protection. Not that it would last long if either were put to the question. The king sanctioned torture these days, and few tongues could not be loosed with enough pain.

His wife seemed to read his mind. "How long before one of the Hundred betrays you all? One person can undo all that you have done."

"You're right," he replied. "Yet still, every man I chose is a man of courage and patriotism. Their loyalty is to the realm and its people. Not our despot of a king. And also, we have all sworn the blood oath."

Norla's frown deepened. "Fool man. Ale is stronger than blood. A few glasses at a bad time could have a man whisper what should not be spoken to the wrong man."

"There will be no more," Menendil said. "One hundred men is enough, and the risk of one of them speaking is low."

His wife put a glass in a rack and took up another one to polish.

"Maybe. But what if one of the men you *trust* is already a spy for the king?"

Menendil understood that. He knew the risk, and he knew that establishing the Hundred in the first place was far riskier than maintaining it. If he had chosen poorly, it would be all over before it began.

"If that were so, we would already be dead," he said.

She frowned at him even more strongly, and placed the glass in the rack with great enough force that several heads turned to look at her because of the noise.

She waited until they went back to their muted conversations before she replied.

"Have you considered that they may be waiting to find out all the names of the Hundred?"

Menendil had indeed considered that. He knew it might be possible, but if so he had planned for it. He himself would be betrayed, and ten others. But that was all. One man in ten was a leader, and the men he commanded was not known to the other ten leaders. Only Menendil himself knew them all, and he kept a tiny vial of deadly poison in his boot. If he were captured, he would kill himself. That way the Hundred would be kept safe. At least, if he had the courage to do what must be done.

Norla gave up polishing glasses and took a cloth from her apron to wipe over the bar.

"I hear tell that the saddler's son up the street turned in his own father for talking about the seventh knight." She whispered those last words so softly that he could barely hear it.

"I heard the same story," he replied quietly, wiping down the bar next to her. "Only both father and son were talking about it, and it was the apprentice that turned them in. The king's men spread the word that it was the son in order to encourage relations to report on one another."

That was what he had heard anyway. It was hard to know the truth these days. It was hard at any time, but things were worse than they ever had been before, and they would deteriorate further.

"That may be. But either way, secrets will out, as they say."

He knew she was right. He played a dangerous game right now. Worse, he did not know if there was even a point in it. But he *did* believe in the prophecy. He just hoped the seventh knight would show up soon. The longer things went on, the greater the chance that Norla's fears would be realized.

It was at that moment that the door to the inn opened, and his heart thudded in his chest. Beside him, Norla stilled, then her hand recommenced swiping the cloth over the bar.

A soldier entered the room, young and dangerous looking. Following him came four others. They were well dressed, their uniforms new and their boots shiny. But they had not been in the army long. These men were mercenaries, gathered from off the streets to swell the king's army. They had none of the look to them of trained military men, yet that made them all the more dangerous.

Menendil glanced casually at Norgril in the corner. He suddenly appeared drunk, half asleep in his chair. But that was an act. His hand hung loosely in his lap, right next to the hilt of his sword.

The soldiers entered the room, an air of arrogance to them. They looked about, and the inn was suddenly deathly quiet. The young men in the corner looked nervous. No doubt they regretted, at least for the moment, whatever misdemeanors they had been up to last night. Guilt exuded from them, but Menendil did not think they had any reason to be worried. If anything, they were just the type the king was looking to recruit into the army rather than punish.

In the silence of the room, the footfalls of the soldiers' boots were loud as they came toward the bar, looking everyone over as they did so.

Menendil took a deep breath. If the worst happened, he was not too old to defend himself. He had not forgotten his training, and Norgril he could count on. His wife would make an account of herself too. She had more than one knife on her body, and she knew how to use them. That was necessary when working in an inn, at least from time to time. Though showing the blade had always been enough.

It would not be for these men though.

10. Words of Power

The days atop the mountain passed, and Faran and Ferla prospered in their training. Asana remained somewhat cool and distant. But they did not think that was because he was displeased with them. Something weighed on his mind, and he seldom spoke at length to anyone but Kubodin.

This place was very different from the valley. Faran's heart remained there, within the little cabin and by the lake. Yet still, he had begun to like the mountain more and more each day. The peace here was wonderful, and the thought that the immortal elves were not far away was intriguing. Asana said they never ventured beyond their forest, but Kubodin said he had seen them once as a company of them marched by the foot of the mountain on some errand. He had seen them, but not spoken to them.

Faran and Ferla still practiced with their bows. But they did not hunt. Neither Asana nor Kubodin ate meat, and there was plenty of food available from the gardens Kubodin tended.

Their skill at sword-fighting increased. Yet their gains now were slow. It was always thus, Faran knew, and Asana confirmed it. The better at a skill you got, the slower gains in expertise became. But this was where mastery was attained. For those who could push themselves hard, those slight improvements did come, and in a fight that was the difference between life and death.

And the both of them pushed themselves, earning even Kubodin's grudging respect. He seldom gave praise, but he watched their practice from time to time and grinned at them in approval. Once, he even bowed to them when they had finished sparring.

"Those knights had better be as good as legend claims," he said. "Else they'll be in for trouble they can't handle."

Faran's heart surged at that, but Kareste's reply sobered him.

"They *are* as good as legend claims, and some better."

It was not what either Faran or Ferla wanted to hear, but the truth was all that mattered. Sweet lies would kill them. Pride would destroy them. Only the truth would save them, so they trained harder still and even Asana seemed surprised. But however hard they trained, he had more to teach them, and they realized how truly skilled he was. Beside him, they were fumbling amateurs.

Ferla was better than Faran, as she always had been. But not drastically so, and when they sparred he could sometimes win.

Their training changed after a few months though. Not with Asana, but with Kareste. For, as she warned them, the knights did not fight with weapons of steel alone.

"I cannot teach the way Aranloth did, by laying my mind over yours. I don't have his skill. But you don't need that now. You have the feeling of magic inside yourselves, and we will fan those flames."

Faran could tell that she did not like admitting a lack of skill. If lack of skill it was. How many other lòhrens could do what Aranloth had done? He was not sure, but he suspected it was few. Or none.

So it was that they trained with Asana until noon, and then after lunch with Kareste until the stars sprang in the sky.

She taught them more words of power, concentrating on those that could be used in battle. But mostly, they were defensive magics, for that was the foundation of attack. Only when you were secure could you bring the fight to the enemy. Doing so before then was to risk life on a gamble.

Late one afternoon when the shredded clouds across the sky were turning pink before the oncoming night, they practiced just such a thing.

Kareste stood before Faran, staff raised, a tongue of faint blue fire darting from its tip.

Durnwah, he proclaimed, though he was getting better at using words of power by thought alone instead of saying them aloud.

This was the word for shield, and a green dome of wavery light flared before him. Kareste's magic struck it and slipped away.

Faran staggered back, surprised. This was the first time that a shield had appeared when he uttered the word of power. A proper shield, at any rate. Before then it had been tattered filaments of light like ribbons in the air before they fragmented and fell apart.

"Excellent!" cried Kareste. "Keep it together!"

Even as he looked he saw that the shield had begun to fade, so he concentrated again and uttered durnwah once more, this time under his breath. The shield strengthened, and it was perhaps even stronger than it had been before.

Kareste stepped toward him. Blue fire darted from her staff again, this time toward the lower edge of the shield. With his mind, he imagined the shield a little larger, and it expanded at his thought.

The two forces met each other. Her fire flashed away and disappeared. But it was stronger than it had been before, and this time he felt something vast behind it. It was, he thought, her will, and he realized how much she was holding back her power. Yet the Kingshield Knights would not have her skill, and he sensed that using magic in this way was like a muscle. The more it was used the stronger it became. So he could improve.

Again and again Kareste attacked him, moving around and forcing him to raise the shield, or lower it, or form it behind him.

And he beat her off, even if she was not employing her full power. But he grew weary, and the shield eventually dimmed and then flickered out like a candle gutted by the wind.

She came to a standstill and leaned on her staff. "You did well, Faran. Very well indeed."

"But the shield failed me."

"So it did, but all magics have limits. It's no different than running, or swinging an axe or enduring cold or heat. The body and the mind have breaking points. You have learned more in months than some lòhrens in years. Don't despair at that. Rejoice, for you have a greater gift at magic than any of the knights."

"Yet they have the greater practice and experience."

She nodded at that. "Do not forget it. But do not underestimate yourself either. They fear you, and Ferla. Otherwise, they would not seek your death."

Ferla's turn came next, and Kareste pressed her hard. Even as Ferla was better with swords, so Faran was better with magic. She could not match what he had done, yet still she conjured a shield of sorts, and held it for a while.

When they were done, night had fallen and they walked the little distance back to Danath Elbar. Kubodin stood at the entrance, and a smile hovered on his lips.

"Better to trust steel than magic," he said.

Kareste pursed her lips. "A strange thing for *you* to say."

The little man seemed surprised at that, but he said nothing.

Faran was surprised too. The words seemed to indicate that Kubodin had use of magic, but there had never been any indication of that, and the little man seemed the most unlikely type to delve into such arts.

Kubodin drew his axe from its belt loop. "See this?" he asked raising the wicked weapon high. "It's all I need, and it has a name. Do you know what it is?"

"No," Ferla said, curious.

"Ha! Tricked you. It has two names, in fact." He tilted the left blade of the axe toward them. "This blade is called Spite." Then he tilted the right blade toward them next. "This is Malice. And do you know what their name is together in my language?"

They did not, and he knew it, for he did not wait on an answer.

"Discord!" He proclaimed. "It's an ancient weapon of my people, handed down through long generations even as Asana's sword was. It's even said a spirit dwells in the axe. If so, it's one crazy spirit. But I like him! He enjoys a good fight!"

Kubodin slid the haft back through the loop and wandered down the tunnel ahead of them without saying anything more.

Ferla grinned. "I *like* that man," she whispered.

"There is more to him than he shows," Kareste answered. "But don't heed his words about magic. It can be unreliable. But it's the same with anything. Get to know it. Master it. It'll serve you well when it's most needed." She pointed her staff at their swords. "Don't forget there's magic in your blades and armor as well. Its nature is different, and you have no control over it, but it's invaluable."

Faran had not forgotten. Of late, his own skill with magic had grown, but he knew he would need every advantage he could get, and he would be forever grateful to Aranloth for giving him both sword and armor.

Ferla must have been thinking just as he was. "I miss Aranloth," she said.

"We all do," Kareste replied. "But we'll miss him more before this is done."

11. You are Beyond Good

Asana came at him, his thin sword a ribbon of bright death in the early-morning air. Faran spun away, trying to avoid him but also Kubodin coming in from the side.

They both sparred him today, and he felt the pressure of facing not just two opponents, but two who were skilled beyond the dreams of most warriors.

Kubodin often watched, though rarely joined the training sessions. But today Asana had called him over and asked him to put aside his axe and participate. For that, Faran was grateful. The axe was the little man's weapon of choice, and he would have been even more dangerous with it. Yet it was not very suitable for sparring, although Faran knew he must learn to face all sorts of weapons.

Instead of the axe, Kubodin had retrieved a broadsword from the stockpile of weapons that they used in their training. It was not a gentleman's weapon as was Asana's blade. It was thick and heavy, and it was used to bash through armor, helms and shields.

Yet the wiry little man still used it with incredible skill. He should not have had the strength to use such a heavy weapon with so great accuracy and dexterity, but it was not the only surprising thing.

Kubodin had taken off his nondescript tunic, and sparred with a bare chest. Sweat glistened over his taut skin, and there was not a shred of fat on his hard body. But that same skin was scarred in many places. Swords and daggers had taken their toll. There was, perhaps, an axe wound over one of his bony shoulders too. But there were other marks also, and Faran did not think they came from blades at all. They were the claw and bite marks of some beast, and a ferocious animal it must have been.

But Kubodin was here, and that meant his enemies were dead.

Asana reached him first though, that thin ribbon of steel flashing through the air. Faran deflected it with Crane Arcs its Wings, a technique he had learned from Asana and liked. It suited his long arms.

Sparks flashed from the blades. He had not quite got the move right, for there should have been less solid contact. Yet Asana was quick, and what almost worked with him would fully work with someone less skilled.

Faran tried a counterattack. Moving into The Swallow Dips Low, he sunk his bodyweight and struck toward Asana's knees. Almost, he thought he would strike the man and began to pull his blow. But he should have known better.

Asana's blade came down at the last moment, perfectly deflecting his strike and flicking back toward Faran's throat. He staggered away, losing his balance.

It was not graceful. And it sent him into the path of Kubodin whose heavy blade lumbered through the air toward his head. Slower than Asana's, but deadly for the force behind it, that blade might even kill him despite his helm.

Yet again, he somehow staggered out of the way and maneuvered so they could only come at him one at a time.

This type of sparring was dangerous. The weapons were real, even if they all held back from their full speed and strength. Especially Asana. Yet it was a risk worth taking. It was not possible to learn how to fight without sparring. Wooden weapons were the beginning of this, but being of wood and not deadly it could not simulate a real fight. The fear was not there. The edge of wariness was not built. Confidence against a true opponent was not grown.

And despite the fact that Faran was losing here, his confidence soared. Asana was perhaps the greatest swordsman alive. Kubodin was greatly skilled, maybe even better than the Kingshield Knights. They attacked him together, and he was still holding them off.

As he edged to the side again, trying to stop them both coming at him at once, always trying to make one opponent get in the way of the other, he caught a glimpse of Ferla.

She stood well to the side, out of their practice area. But her eyes were wide and there was concern on her face. She worried for him, even as he had worried for her before when it had been her turn.

He decided to take the attack to Asana. Driving forward in Tempest Blows the Dust, he pressed home the momentary advantage he had bought by catching his opponent between himself and Kubodin.

Asana showed no emotion. He could have been strolling through the gardens, yet his eyes narrowed and he deftly sidestepped, avoiding both Faran's attack and bumping into Kubodin.

But that cleared the way for Kubodin to race in, which he did with a bloodcurdling scream.

It was startling, and Faran knew intuitively its purpose. It was designed to intimidate and instill fear. But he was having none of that.

He sidestepped to the left, angling now to keep Kubodin between him and Asana, and lunged forward with a stabbing motion.

Kubodin checked his advance and smashed his broadsword down against Faran's blade. There was a mighty crash of steel against steel, but Faran was already moving.

Whipping his blade up in a loop he struck for Kubodin's neck.

And he pulled the blow, for Kubodin had not reacted in time and would have been dead in a real fight.

Kubodin looked stunned, then withdrew laughing wildly.

"Hey! Good work!" he called out.

But the sparring was not over. Asana came forward nimbly, the point of his blade circling in the air. This was a trick intended to shift an opponent's attention onto the blade and away from the hips and shoulders which usually signaled when an attack was initiated.

So it was that Faran was not caught by surprise when Asana dropped low and slashed sideways with his blade. Yet the move was still blindingly quick and he only just managed to step back and avoid it.

But in his haste to retreat, he stumbled and fell. Asana pounced on him, swift as a plummeting hawk, and Faran found the tip of the other man's blade hovering next to his neck before he could even think about scrambling to his feet or even defending himself from the ground.

A moment Asana stood above him, then he stepped away and smoothly sheathed his sword. He leaned forward and helped Faran to his feet.

"You did well," Asana congratulated him. "I dare say Kubodin was surprised."

Kubodin shuffled forward, pulling his tunic back on over his head.

"Just in case anyone is interested, the sword is *not* my favored weapon. With an axe, well that's a different matter."

"Peace, my friend," Asana said. "You were beaten, and that is an end to it. When he can beat you regularly with the sword, then you can change to the axe. That should make for some interesting sparring."

Faran did not want to do that. Kubodin was greatly skilled, but pulling a blow from an axe in sparring was very difficult, and that would make it even more dangerous than what they had just done. But he would not improve unless he pushed himself.

Ferla came over, and she was grinning. She put her arms around him and kissed him on the cheek, something that she had never done before.

"Well done, Faran," she said quietly.

Kubodin was not so quiet. He whistled loudly and slapped his thighs.

Ferla arched an eyebrow at him. "What's so amusing?"

"Hey! Why should he get the hugs? I'm the one that nearly died."

Ferla eyed him a moment, then she stepped forward and hugged him, also kissing him on the cheek.

The little man went quiet, but for the first time that Faran had seen Asana laughed himself, and his eyes lit up with mirth.

Kubodin's tanned face turned red, and he walked off muttering to himself in a language they had never heard.

Faran was amazed at the transformation in Asana. But as swiftly as the mirth had come, it disappeared. He was his calm self again, showing nothing on his face. But there was a lightness to his movements as he drew his sword again.

"Come. Let Kubodin alone. You have both won battles there, for he is not easily embarrassed. But he was not expecting that." He glanced at Faran. "Nor you, I suspect. But our training is not done."

"What will we do now?" Faran asked.

"Now, you will both attack me. You have earned the right."

So saying, he edged toward them with soft steps, looking like some predator out of nature, at the one time both eternally patient and also ready to leap into attack.

Ferla drew her sword, and a look of determination masked her face now. This was the warrior Ferla, and the huntress he had known in Dromdruin valley was gone.

Faran moved to the side, trying to situate Asana so that he was surrounded. But the swordsman moved even as he did, the tip of his blade flickering out in a slice that nearly had Faran, but even as the blade cut the air near his neck the master pivoted and struck out at Ferla.

She barely stopped the blow, bringing her sword up at the last moment to inelegantly block the strike.

Asana followed up the attack, his sword a blur, and Ferla retreated. She did not back away in a straight and predictable line, but instead zigzagged. It was to no avail.

Asana's sword rang against the top of her helm. It could just as easily have been a killing stroke to her unprotected neck. But even as that blow landed he rolled to the ground, avoided Faran's own attack and leaped toward him.

The man was a blur of speed. Faran barely saw the blow that rang against his own helm, and he did not see at all the simultaneous kick that struck his knee. The first would have been lethal, but the second was dangerous too. It was nothing more than a light tap, but it was at such an angle that it could have torn the joint apart if delivered with power. That would also prove fatal in a swordfight, for a man who stood on one leg could not prevail against an agile attacker.

It was silent atop the mountain, and only the whispering breeze through the garden could be heard. Faran could not believe how fast Asana was, and a glance at Ferla revealed that she too was in awe of the man.

Into the silence, Kareste spoke. No one had seen her approach.

"Aranloth told me how good you were. But he misspoke. You are beyond good."

Asana tilted his head in acknowledgement of the compliment.

"Am I a match for Brand though?"

"Perhaps. But he is a hard man to beat. And he has use of magic."

"But he would not use it against such as I, who cannot defend against it?"

"No, he would never do that."

"I thought not. A pity that all men are not like him."

The look of sadness that so often seemed to come to Asana's face was there now, stronger than ever. Faran wondered what the cause was, and if there was anything he could do to help.

12. Live or Die

Clouds wreathed the mountain top, and there was a chill in the air despite it being midsummer. But Nuril Faranar, the Lonely Watchman, remained as unpredictable as all mountains were.

Even as Faran and Ferla jogged down a steep track on the southern slope, the clouds gave way and the bright morning sun shone upon them. Yet the grass was slick with dew, and they were wary of their footing.

This grew worse. Only a little while later, the clouds returned and a drizzle of rain fell. This was accompanied by a piercing breeze that cut through their armor like ice and chilled them to the bone.

But they were fit and strong, and they ran on, if more slowly so they could pick their steps on the wet grass with care.

Asana did not believe much in running to stay fit. "A fight that cannot be won in the first few moments is one in which you may die," he had told them often enough. "Skill outweighs fitness by a factor of a thousand to one."

They did not disagree with him. But they loved to run, and remaining fit also meant they could practice sword patterns and spar for longer periods, which quickened their training in the end.

They had done all that early this morning, and Asana had let them go for the run they desired. But there would be more training for them when they returned.

The clouds parted again, and the wind dropped. Rain still fell for a while out of a seemingly blue sky, but it too soon passed and the air felt fresh and alive.

Southward, the smudge of forest on the far horizon that was Halathar became clear. Faran longed to walk amid those trees, for the forest was a matter of legend, and it was said many fair creatures of the old world yet lived there that had died out in the rest of Alithoras. He did not think it would ever happen though, for he had other strings pulling him toward a different fate.

They did not go too far down the mountain. It was a day's climb back up again, nor did they wish to delay their training with Asana, and after him with Kareste. So they stopped on a green patch of grass overshadowed by an oak tree, one of the few they had ever seen on the mountain.

The cold had stunted the tree's growth, but it looked to Faran to be an old, old tree. Its leafy boughs provided shelter from the rain that threatened to return, and the gnarled trunk was large enough that they could both sit down together and lean their backs against it.

"It's strange," Ferla said. "In a way I feel at home. I've never been here before, but my ancestors lived all around. They knew these lands like we knew Dromdruin, and called them home. Somehow, though I can't explain it, I feel a part of that."

Faran looked out at the view. He had felt something similar to her, but had not found words to describe it as well as she had. It was an eerie feeling of coming home to a place he had never been.

"I know what you mean," he said thoughtfully. "It's not just that our ancestors lived and died here. They fought wars here, faced creatures of the Shadow far greater and darker than anything we have seen ourselves. Sorcery was unleashed upon them. And somehow they survived. They changed here under those influences, and all that they became was born right here, in this very place."

Ferla leaned against him as she often did, shoulder to shoulder.

"We have a lot to live up to, don't we?"

It was true. Somehow, they had become a link in the long fight against evil. Their ancestors had started it, but it continued now. By some quirk of fate they had become involved with a figure of legend like Aranloth, and with a lòhren like Kareste. On the other side were creatures of sorcery and knights.

"Do you believe in destiny?" Ferla asked quietly.

"I'm not sure. Maybe. It seems to me though that a person makes their own destiny. But do they really make it, or are their choices foreordained and they only think they make them?"

Ferla sighed. "Answering a question with other questions isn't a straight answer."

He laughed. "Well, what do you think?"

She leaned in a little closer. "Aranloth told me this, once. He said that a house had walls and windows and a roof. But it was the person who walked in through the door and lived there that made it into a home. He claimed destiny was like that. Circumstances created a need for a certain thing to happen, and someone stepped into the role."

Faran thought on that. It was not something the old man had ever said to him, but he sensed Aranloth's attitude in it.

"That seems as good as any way of looking at it, I suppose. Why the sudden interest in destiny though?"

She looked away. "There you go again, asking questions instead of giving opinions. When will you commit yourself to a solid answer?"

He laughed at that, but it did occur to him that she had just done the same thing. She had avoided his question by asking one of her own.

They sat in companionable silence for a while.

Farther down the slope, a fox emerged from a group of shrubs and trotted without haste, but obvious determination, on some errand known only to it. The creature's red coat was darkened by water, more likely picked up from slinking through the grass than directly from any rain.

"Going back to its den after the night's hunt," Ferla whispered.

That was likely true. No doubt it had covered a lot of ground as well, maybe even stalking the lower slopes because there were more food sources for it there than on this part of the mountain.

The fox entered a slight gulley, barely visible from where they watched, and was gone from sight. It did not emerge again, and Faran hoped it had found its home. He wished too that one day he would find his own.

Ferla ran her hand back and forth down the leather of her boot, a gesture she often made when she was content. But it abruptly stopped, and a few moments later she spoke.

"How long before they find us again?" she asked.

Faran knew who she meant. Lindercroft would not stop hunting them. All the more so because they had escaped him twice. There was something personal between them now, some fight that would never cease until either he or they had won. Nor would the king leave them alone.

"I don't know," he answered. "But I feel what you feel. It's coming. One day, somehow, they'll find us and what was begun in Dromdruin will be finished."

"You make it sound like we'll lose."

He took hold of her hand in his own. "I didn't mean that. I just meant that we'll fight them again, especially Lindercroft."

"And what then, Faran? Will we win?"

He did not answer straight away. To her, he could only tell the truth. He needed no vow, no promise, to know that. She was who she was and he respected her. There would only *ever* be the truth between them.

"I don't know. But neither do they. They fear us, Ferla. Why, I'm not sure. But they do, and we've learned things. Swords and lòhrengai, steel to counter steel and magic to offset sorcery. Live or die, we'll fight them. And just maybe we're already ready. But they haven't found us yet, and every day we grow in skill."

"I'm not sure, Faran. Sometimes I feel invincible. Other days I fear them." She leaned in even closer.

"Whatever happens, we'll be together. I fear them too, but I promise, they fear us just as much."

It was time that they got back to running, but just now Faran did not want to go anywhere. He felt close to Ferla, even closer than normal.

"Have you changed your mind about being the seventh knight?" she asked unexpectedly.

It was something he had thought about deeply. Without doubt, Faladir needed the seventh knight.

"Nothing has changed for me. I'll oppose Lindercroft and the king with everything I have. I'll try to bring justice for Dromdruin. But I hate the knights for what they did to my grandfather. I could never become one myself."

Ferla nodded at that. He hoped she understood, but the look on her face was unreadable just then.

They looked out in silence a little while longer at the world below, but clouds were drawing in again and it was time to be up and running. If it rained heavily, it would be an unpleasant run back to the top of the mountain.

Ferla led them on the way back, her long strides sure and easy, and her body lithe and graceful even beneath the hindering armor.

The wet grass hampered them, and the steepness of the slope made running a grueling task. Yet they persisted, moving slowly and surely. Rain began to fall again, and with it a wind that lashed at them.

It grew dark, and distant thunder rumbled. If there was a storm now, they might need to take their metal armor off and seek cover. It was dangerous enough to run up a steep slope, let alone if lightning began to flash.

The rain grew heavier, and rills of water leaped down the slope. Ferla nimbly jumped one, and Faran followed. But even as he landed Ferla spun and grabbed him, pulling him to the ground.

He did not know why, but he trusted her. She drew her sword, and he did likewise, seeking out enemies ahead of them. But there was no one there.

She hunkered down low, and Faran realized she was not looking ahead as was he, but upward. He followed her gaze, and dread settled over him colder than wind and rain.

It was high above, and speeding through a wrack of twisting clouds, but it was an elù-drak that he saw, and for a moment he thought all was lost. But the creature was flying swiftly, perhaps to escape the sudden storm, and it did not seem to have seen them.

In moments, the thing was gone, swallowed by the roiling clouds and curtains of rain. They waited a little while longer, but saw no further sign of it.

"Best to use the cover of this storm while it lasts," Ferla said. He agreed, and they began to run again, swifter than before and glancing skyward often.

Faran was sure they had not been seen. But it was a close thing. The enemy still sought them out, and had it been bright and sunny they may well have been observed. The stabbing fear that still pounded with each heartbeat made him question what he had told Ferla just before. Were they ready to face their enemies?

13. The Lure of the Stone

Druilgar sat upon the throne of Faladir. He wore his armor. He *always* wore his armor since a faceless member of a crowd had sped an arrow toward him. The fool had got away, but where there was one fool there were others.

One of them stood before him now. He was a pompous thing, talking too much and constantly wording things to make himself sound good and his actions effective.

They had not been. Not fully, anyway. Yet the man was loyal. He had been handpicked for the job too. The previous Captain of the City Guard had retired. Too old he had said, but Druilgar had known he did not have the heart for what must be done. This man had been recommended to take his place. He had the heart, but not quite the wit.

"What of the rebellion?" Druilgar asked.

That brought the captain's ramblings to an end.

"The rebellion?"

"Did you not hear me?"

The man cleared his throat and looked suddenly nervous.

"That is, er, totally dealt with. There never was much of a rebellion, just a few words whispered here and there. Those that did so have been, er, punished appropriately."

The king knew what that punishment was. He had set it, but apparently his new Captain of the City Guard did not like to use the words torture and murder. That was of no account, for whether he said the words or not he certainly carried out the deeds.

"What you say is not quite true, captain. Not all those who rebel are caught. Not all those who defy me state it openly. Yet I know they whisper against me in private. Your spies have not ferreted them all out. Is that not so?"

The man hesitated. He chose wisely though, acknowledging the truth.

"There are those who speak against you, I'm sure. There are always those who are jealous and foolish. But their numbers are low."

Druilgar was not so sure of that. "And what are you doing to find them?"

"As you know, I have spies everywhere. Soldiers not dressed as soldiers. Commoners who are known to be loyal. If a whisper is spoken we'll hear it."

All this, Druilgar knew. "It's not enough. Send out more spies. Have soldiers question people in the street and their place of work. There remains resistance, and I want to stamp it out. Not even a whisper should be uttered. Nor even a thought born in bed at night with no one to hear. Do you understand?"

The captain bowed. "It will be as you command."

"Do this also. Have soldiers march the streets in great numbers. Let them be loud and obvious. Let no one think that this city isn't under my rule. That will send a message that I have the means to detect and punish disobedience."

"It will be done, sire."

"I know it will, or you will answer to me. Now go, I have other matters to deal with."

The captain left, and he hid his fear well. But it was there, and Druilgar sensed it. If he had not, he would have had the man killed. A servant who did not live in fear did not carry out orders efficiently.

There was another man in the room. He had remained silent throughout the briefing, but he stepped closer to the throne now. His helm was tucked under one arm, and he bowed.

Druilgar considered him. As a knight, Sofanil was known to him. Yet only at a superficial level. The man was a mystery, deeper than the other knights and harder to read.

For all the time they had spent together, Druilgar knew him as well as or better than anyone living. Yet not well enough. His thoughts were his own, and he never quarreled or disputed. What he thought of the other knights, no one knew. He remained humble and enigmatic. Yet Druilgar guessed. The man was loyal to him, yet he probably held the other knights in disdain. He was not the most senior among them. Far from it. Yet his mind was quicker, and perhaps his sword too. But in one such as he, ambition ruled. All the more so because he hid it.

Yet still, the man served well, and that should be rewarded. He was *not* the most senior knight, but that could change.

"The captain was scared," Druilgar said. "But he hid it. That is good, but do you think he is capable of fulfilling his duties?"

Sofanil cocked his head. "You appointed him, sire. You would not have done so if you thought someone else could perform better."

Druilgar felt a shiver of fear. This man was smart. He was a threat. He never said anything that was unsuitable, and his answer just now, which was no answer, proved it. Those words could never be held against him, for even if the captain failed, Sofanil had ventured no opinion but merely supported his king's decision.

Yet the man was loyal, at least so far as could be determined. So too he was proving extremely capable, which was a trait in short supply. He was a tool to be used to best advantage.

"I am troubled," Druilgar admitted.

Sofanil knew what he meant, which was another trait most becoming in a servant.

"My lord? Do you speak of Lindercroft and Savanest?"

There it was again. He did not seem to infer that his brother knights were incompetent, and yet by asking if they were the cause of the trouble, he sheeted home the problems to them directly. Moreover, he was right to do so.

"That is what I speak of, and Lindercroft especially. He has had more time to carry out his task."

Sofanil spoke slowly, as he always did. "The seventh knight, if such exists, is a threat. There is reason to be troubled, and Lindercroft and Savanest have not yet killed the young man and his companions. That is a task that must be accomplished."

Druilgar stifled the grin that came to his face. He *liked* Sofanil. He had cast aspersions at the other knights, and yet nothing that he said could be construed as false or aggressive. It was merely a summary of indisputable facts, that strung together, happened, if you looked at them in a certain way, to cast extreme doubt over the abilities of his brother knights. But he had not actually said it.

However subtle the attack, it was still an attack. Sofanil was ambitious, and he had just revealed it now.

"What would you do if you were charged with the task?"

Sofanil did not answer straight away. He considered the question carefully, seeking out any trap it might contain.

He was a cautious and thoughtful man, and Druilgar liked that. Yet he did not lack courage, and his was deeper than the brasher kind. When he set his mind to a task, he fulfilled it. If there was danger, he bypassed it but did not let it concern him. If it could not be bypassed, he faced it coolly.

All in all, he was a strange man, and his physical appearance was the least of it. Yet he did look strange.

The man had milk-white skin, paler than any Druilgar had seen before. But his hair was black as jet, and the contrast was startling. It was perhaps some disease he suffered from, though if so it did not affect his mental or physical abilities.

"What I would have done was hold out the hand of friendship. I would have disowned you, in my words to them, and gained their trust. All the more easily could I have eliminated them at my leisure. But I fear that opportunity exists no longer."

Again, it was a subtle put down of his rivals. It would have been the better approach, but Druilgar did not think any dissembling would have fooled Aranloth.

"And now?"

"Now a more direct approach is needed. Finding them is only the first step. These people, peasants though the young man and woman appear to be, have shown skill and courage. They should not be underestimated. I would find them, lock them into place and then bring great forces of sorcery and swords to bear upon them."

Again, he had criticized his brother knights, or at least Lindercroft. Twice the man had found them, and twice they had escaped from him. The message was clear. The enemy had been underestimated.

Druilgar decided it was time to put the man under pressure.

"Are your brother knights incompetent, then?"

Sofanil did not move, but he seemed neither scared nor perturbed.

"They are my brothers. It's not my place, but yours, to judge their competence. I merely state the facts. They have failed so far to remove the threat."

"And do you believe this so called seventh knight is truly a threat?"

Sofanil gave the slightest of shrugs. "Of course. Were there no threat, you would not have spent the time and resources on them that you have. Is that not so?"

This time Druilgar actually laughed. He could not remember the last time he had done so, and it felt strange. How deftly this man avoided being pinned down. It was marvelous to watch.

"I like you, Sofanil. And I will reward you. I now charge you with seeking out these enemies and destroying them. You may take a company of soldiers, if you wish. And if you find and kill them before the others, I will reward you beyond their dreams. But if you forget that you serve me, and through me the new Osahka, your life will be in peril."

Sofanil bowed gracefully. He showed neither pleasure at the opportunity nor chagrin at the threat.

"I will meditate on this, sire. Mayhap I can devise a ruse that will deceive our enemies. If so, I may not use soldiers."

"That choice is yours. This only I ask. Go forth, and bring me their heads. I tire of their existence, and their very lives distract me from the great tasks at hand. Osahka stirs, and the destiny of this nation grows. Nay, the destiny of Alithoras, for the stone is power such as we have never known. With it, I can rule all realms. I can conquer all lands. I can bring all people under my sway, and draw them in unity along the one true way. Osahka leads, and we follow."

Sofanil did not quite smile. He never did. But his eyes lit with an inner light of desire.

"May it be so, sire. Osahka leads, like a great light in the heavens guiding the steps of travelers. By that light, we will cast a mighty shadow over the land, making it ours. And yours will be the first shadow, and this nation you rule, teeming with warriors and swordsmen, the second. And my sword will be among them, always at your service."

Druilgar was pleased. This man saw the vision as did he, and it might be that the stone influenced them both in that.

"Kneel, Sofanil. I will bless you."

The knight adjusted the sword at his side so that he could kneel, and he bowed his head.

Druilgar stood from the throne. He had not intended this, and it would drain his powers to the brink, but it felt right.

He placed his left hand over the other man's head. That jet-black hair was not so black up close. Traces of silver touched it at the temples.

"All men will be our brothers," Druilgar muttered. "All women our sisters. As one the shadow will make us, and under Osahka all will be equal."

It was not quite true. Some, like he and the knights, would be more equal than the others. But that was fitting, for there were always those burdened with leadership.

He felt the magic come to him easily now. Lòhrengai had always been a struggle to embrace. But its brother, elùgai, was sweet as cool water under the blistering sun. It rushed through him easily, and away in the tower he felt the pulse of the stone like a twin heartbeat to his own.

Druilgar formed the will, and the magic obeyed. It leaped through his hand and into Sofanil, changing him. The knight stiffened and screamed. This, Druilgar knew, was painful. But pain was of no account.

Several long moments the magic flared through the other man's body. A trickle of blood seeped out of one ear, and the man trembled beneath his touch.

Then the magic flared out like a gutted candle, and for a moment both men were one in the longing for it to return.

Looking down, Druilgar saw that the silver in that black hair was gone. Not a strand of it remained. Then he staggered back to sit on the throne, for he doubted just then his legs could hold him up.

Likewise, Sofanil sprawled to the ground, gasping, and the helm under his elbow clattered and rolled over the floor.

Slowly the knight brought himself to his knees, and he gathered his helm. Standing once more, he looked at Druilgar, his eyes bright and an emotion in them that might have been awe.

Sofanil drew a deep breath, and he seemed to gather strength. He was younger, stronger, better than he was before. His body was that of a twenty year old, at the peak of physical prowess, yet the mind behind those eyes was that of an experienced and confident warrior.

"You have rewarded me indeed, sire. How shall I thank you?"

Druilgar was exhausted, and he wanted this interview over now. It did no good to be seen as weak, and he could barely sit on the throne.

"Go. Find our enemies and kill them. That is all I ask."

Sofanil bowed, turned on his heels and strode from the throne room. He had been dangerous before, but now he was more so. Just as well that he was loyal, but that was all the worse for their enemies.

Druilgar took some shuddering breaths. He was spent, and now alone. Why was he *always* alone? Why did people shun him? Yet he was stronger without them. To rely on others was to be weak.

The weariness he felt was overpowering, yet stronger by far was the pull of the stone. Osahka would replenish him. For a moment, he tried to resist. It could not be good to need it so much, and he would recover without it. But the lure intensified and he staggered to his feet.

"Guards!" he called to the men stationed at the entrance to the throne room. "Ready my carriage!"

14. Loyal to the King

Menendil slowed his breathing and wiped down the bar, pretending nothing unusual was going on. Fear made a man look guilty, and he knew it, yet it was hard to remain calm when so much was at stake.

The five soldiers spread out, making it their business to mind everyone else's, knowing they instilled fear and enjoying the nervous looks they got from the patrons.

One soldier moved close to Norgril, then snorted in disgust.

"This one's drunker than a farmer on his first trip to town."

Norgril certainly played the part well. Even his eyes seemed blurry, but his hand was still near his sword hilt and the arrogant young man stood no chance against him if it came down to a fight.

Menendil hoped dearly it would not. He could not take the other four soldiers.

Their leader approached him. Out of the corner of his eye Menendil saw the table of youths look uncertain. Some pulled out their chairs as if to go. But one of them shook his head urgently not to do so. They wanted out of here, but to try to leave now was to invite suspicion.

The soldier looked Menendil up and down. It was an arrogant look, and anger started to surge through Menendil rather than fear. These men had no right to come in here and look down on him.

"We've heard this place is full of traitors," the man said.

Menendil stopped wiping the bar. It had been a strange thing to say, especially if the man believed it to be true. If he had, it would have been smarter to bring more men and surround him first before making such an accusation. That he had not indicated he was a fool, or that he was just trying to provoke a reaction to see if anyone looked guilty.

Menendil breathed a little easier. He believed both of those things were true.

"On my honor," Menendil replied. "There are only patriots here, loyal with everything they have to the realm."

"Is that so?"

"Of course, good sir."

The soldier turned to Menendil's wife. "Is that the truth, woman?"

She smiled at the man. "Oh yes. Mender here is an idiot, but he's loyal to a fault. I assure you of that."

The soldier looked around. His expression was suddenly bored.

"What of these others?" He pointed to the youths at the table. "Are they king's men?"

"I've seen no sign otherwise," Menendil replied. "They drink and they pay and never a bad word has come out of their mouth in my hearing."

The soldier glanced at the men he commanded. They too seemed bored. Obviously, they had not noticed anything they should bring his attention to.

"Would you like an ale, fine sir?" Menendil asked. Better to make out that he wanted these soldiers here.

"We're on duty, barkeep," the soldier replied stiffly. "We don't drink when there are traitors to find."

Menendil nodded briskly, hoping he was not overdoing it.

"Of course, fine sir. I wouldn't want to interfere with that. But you see, it's good for business if soldiers are known to drink here. It keeps the riffraff away, and there are always plenty of those. If you stayed, even for just one, on the house mind you, it would show that this was a respectable establishment where ne'er-do-wells were unwelcome and where the king's men were given the honor that's their due."

The man looked like he was about to say no, but one of his men spoke up.

"This is thirsty work, cap. We could all do with a rest, and a sip of something to wash away the dust of the street from our mouths."

Menendil knew from the marks on the leader's uniform that he was a captain, but it was best his own military history did not come out, so he bowed deeply as though impressed by the rank.

"To the bar then men, but one drink only mind. We have plenty of places to be right sharp."

Menendil drew a glass of his worst ale from the tap, and served the captain first. Norla began serving too, but to his chagrin she pulled the ale down from his best keg. These men were not worthy of that, and in his time the leader would never have made the grade as captain. They were nothing more than riffraff themselves, but he let none of his thoughts show and smiled obsequiously.

He glanced at Norgril over in the corner. The man was seemingly asleep now, his head resting in his hands on the table. But he was positioned so that he could open a slit of an eye now and then and assess what was going on. But for now, hearing would be enough. The danger had passed unless someone said the wrong thing.

Norgril was a good man to have around. The best. But the youths were not, and Menendil was glad to see them finally stand up and shuffle their way out.

The soldiers watched them go. They did not say anything, but their eyes narrowed in suspicion. These were men just looking to find fault and to start a fight. They were the worst sort, and should never be given authority or swords. But these were the type of men now favored in the kingdom.

The door closed behind the youths. He pictured them running once outside, and Menendil nodded as though satisfied.

"Good," he said. "They'll spread the word that king's men drink here, and the inn will become known as the place to be."

"More like," the captain disagreed, "they're off to find a lone man in an alley to rob now that drink has given them courage."

It was true, and Menendil marveled how easy it was for a man to find fault with others – the same fault a man possessed himself. For surely the captain was the sort to try robbing a lone man himself, so long as he had a few companions to back him up.

"They did have the look of thieves to them," Menendil muttered. "But their coin spends as well as anyone's. All the more reason though to have such fine gentlemen as yourselves in a place like this. It keeps the peace and attracts better customers. So, if it pleases you, come by anytime and bring your soldiering friends with you. For you at least, the drinks will always be on the house."

That got the man's attention. Menendil could almost see the thoughts spin and buzz in his head. He could do well out of this, and perhaps get free meals too. But while he was thinking these things he was not asking the wrong sort of questions and probing in a way that might reveal guilt.

"Bah! I'm not here to source business for you, barkeep. I have a job to do, and a serious one. Yet it may be that I'll come back from time to time."

The term barkeep was aggravating to Menendil, for he was the proprietor not an employee, but he let that pass. A time of reckoning was coming, and he could wait until then. When the seventh knight came ... but now was not the time to think thoughts like that.

The soldiers ended up drinking another round each, and showed signs of settling in to drink for the rest of the day. But the captain stirred them up, eventually.

"Get to it, slackards!" he cried when they protested his decision to leave. A decision no doubt brought on by fear rather than choice, for the captain would be the one to answer to his superior officer if it were discovered they flouted their duties.

The men took their displeasure out on Norgril as they moved to the door, kicking his chair and seemingly waking him up from a drunken stupor to splutter in surprise.

But he was not surprised, and had they pushed it further several of them would have died in a heartbeat.

Menendil sighed a breath of relief as the soldiers left and the door closed behind them. But no one spoke until he had looked through the window and watched them walk down the street.

"Scum," Norgril muttered, and his eyes seemed no longer blurry but burning with anger.

Menendil knew how he felt. But it was his wife who first spoke.

"You surely will get us killed," she said softly.

"You lied as well as I did, to prevent that," Menendil answered.

"Aye. That's because I know nothing."

"Neither did they," Norgril said. "It was a bluff, and no doubt one they try wherever they go to see how people react."

Norla sniffed. "It was a bluff, *this* time."

Menendil held his peace. She was right, and all three of them knew the risks. But he at least knew that the best place to hide was in plain sight. So where better to head the rebellion from than in a bar where the king's men drank and that was under the shadow of the Tower of the Stone itself, and beneath the king's very own nose?

15. Accept Death

Atop Nuril Faranar, the mountain weather was raging even as Faran watched.

They were on the plateau, but at a part they seldom went to. On the northern side, near a sharp drop down from the peak was a flat area of stone rather than grass. It was like a table, flat and smooth, but as large as their normal training area.

And it was for training that Asana had brought them here, yet that training was different from anything they had done before.

"Training," the master had told them, "is empty unless it has the characteristics of a real fight. You must feel under pressure. Circumstances must work against you. You must know *fear*, and deal with it. In this way a similitude to a real fight is achieved, and the training acquires shape and purpose."

Faran certainly felt fear now. What they were doing was dangerous. They had just begun to spar again after a short rest, and the stone beneath their feet as they fought was slick with moisture. At any moment one or the other might slip. More likely him, for Asana seemed poised as ever despite the conditions. But a slip while razor-sharp blades whirred through the air could mean death. Yet still they carried on. This was the realm their training had entered; a place where they pushed each other to the limits.

At least, Faran was pushed to his limit, and therefore grew in skill. Asana was beyond his measure. Sparring Ferla, Faran knew what her skill was and that it was more than his own. But he could see where and by how much. Battling Asana was like looking into a lake whose bottom could not be fathomed.

It was not just the slick stone and razor-like blades that made this dangerous. The sharp drop to one side was steep enough that falling probably meant death. Yet there was also a buffeting wind that came and went and came again in unexpected gusts. With it was a driving whirl of clouds that brought little rain, yet they still roiled and shifted like a fog, but not like any Faran had seen before.

They were in the midst of clouds themselves as they fought, for the top of the mountain was wreathed by a storm. Fortunately, there was no lightning. Yet. But goosebumps prickled on Faran's skin and he was alive to every movement. For every movement might mean death.

The shifting clouds parted momentarily, like a curtain, and Asana, only half visible before, suddenly leaped at him.

Faran dropped low, seeking to avoid the blade and maintain his balance, but Asana deftly adjusted the angle of his attack and steel rang against steel.

Moving forward into attack, Faran sent Asana into retreat, and somehow the man managed to look nimble in circumstances where most people would struggle even to walk.

As quickly as he dared, Faran pressed his attack and Asana backed up toward the steep drop. But the man was full of surprises, and with a slash that turned out to be a feint, he dived and rolled to the side, coming up level with Faran and then darting behind him so that somehow Faran now had his own back to the deadly drop.

It was a killing move in a real fight. He had been set up to be driven off the cliff. Worse, he realized that Asana had lured him into it from the beginning, pretending to be backed away toward the drop himself only so that he could maneuver as he had done and reverse their positions.

From off to the side, Faran heard Ferla gasp. Whether it was in fear for his position, or at Asana's incredible skill at reversing their positions, he was not sure.

But there was no give in Faran. He could call the sparring off with a word or gesture, but he would not. Instead, he attacked.

Momentarily, Asana seemed surprised. But he moved swiftly enough to deflect the blow. Only, it was a feint just as his own had been a little while before.

Faran attempted what his teacher had done, leaping and rolling and coming to his feet again in one swift motion. He had not done it as neatly as Asana, and he had slipped during the process, yet still he had done it all with speed and agility. He was also well-positioned to fend off any blows if they came.

Leaping and rolling was one thing. Coming to his feet and being ready to fight was another. A skilled enemy would be able to kill him there while he was vulnerable if he had not moved with speed and brought his guard up again. But he had done so.

Not quickly enough, however. Asana had backed away from the edge himself, ensuring that they now faced each other with the drop to their side rather than Asana with his back to it.

To Faran's surprise, his mentor lowered his sword and laughed. It was such a rare thing to see.

"Well done, Faran. We'll call that a draw," he said after a few moments.

Faran did not think it was quite a draw. Asana could have had him in that brief moment where he slipped. Another opponent might not have been quick enough to take advantage of that, but Asana was. He had held back.

It was something Asana did. He pushed students to their limits in order that they might learn, yet he did not overwhelm them with his superior skill, which would be demotivating.

Asana must have sensed his doubt. "Truly, it was a genuine contest. I don't say that lightly."

"Thank you, master." Faran and Ferla had taken to calling the man master as was traditional in the lands of the Cheng. It was not quite the same as Osahka, but it was similar.

"Your turn!" Asana called out to Ferla. He unbelted his sword though and picked two spears from the pile of weapons near where they trained. One of them, he threw to Ferla, and she grasped it out of the air with deft skill.

"Swords are the best," he said. "But all the weapons teach you better how to move. All the more so due to their differences. You must adapt, and adapting is learning."

Faran stepped out of the way. He was glad his turn was done, and he wished to be inside and out of this foul weather. But nothing could have prevented him from watching this. Ferla was good with the spear, and Asana, though skilled in everything he did, was the least skilled with the long weapons of spear, staff and halberd.

The wind picked up again, and a spattering of rain pelted at them. The two combatants circled each other, weapons before them and gazes like the eyes of eagles.

Ferla struck first. The tip of the spear drove forward toward Asana's neck. He, and Aranloth also, taught them always to attack the vital areas. And with accuracy. The difference between hitting an opponent on the neck or the top of the shoulder was all the difference in the world.

Asana flicked his spear out, the metal point coming into contact with Ferla's shaft and deflecting it. This was the harder way to stop an attack. It was easier to use shaft against shaft because it gave more leeway for inaccuracy.

Yet this way, it left a counterattack more open, and he used it.

The tip of his spear ran down the shaft toward her fingers, but Ferla was ready and she rolled the spear over bringing it atop Asana's and knocking his down.

Once more she stabbed the weapon forward, this time striking toward the groin.

Asana leaped back, taken by surprise with the speed of her recovery, and only just in time. She had nearly had him.

The master stepped back, and momentarily slipped on the slick stone. It was no feint. Ferla darted forward, her spear slashing this time crosswise in a move intended to hit her opponent's arm. This he managed to block, but it was only just in time and it was no deflection as he preferred but a block of shear strength.

Asana regained his balance, but Ferla pressed her attack home while she had the advantage. Desperately, but silently, Faran cheered her on. She deserved a victory, for her skill was great and her courage greater to spar under these circumstances.

Their spears cracked like whips and rattled with the force of block and parry, for they both attacked hard. This was not the graceful sparring that usually made up their training but a ferocious fight, only just a little way short of actual combat.

The skill was incredible to watch, and Faran envied Ferla. She was as good with a spear as a sword, and she moved with the same deadly grace that Asana did.

The master struck forward, the tip of the spear darting like a viper's tongue, but Ferla had already evaded the blow before it was halfway delivered, her shaft slamming down on Asana's and knocking it from his grip to rattle on the stone beneath their feet.

She was already moving though before her opponent's weapon hit the ground. The point of her own spear rested now at Asana's throat.

They stood perfectly still for a moment. Faran's heart soared, and the wind buffeted them all driving a squall of rain before it.

Ferla withdrew the spear, and Asana bowed to her. Despite his wet clothes and the foul weather, he still looked poised as ever.

"You beat me, Ferla. And it has been long since that has happened, although Kubodin pushes me hard at times."

Ferla seemed shocked. "I really did, didn't I?"

"Indeed." He gestured Faran to join them. "You have both learned quickly," he continued. "More quickly than most that I have taught before, and some of those were very gifted. Be proud of yourselves. Your skill is above that of ordinary warriors. You are now in a group of elite fighters, and your names will spread over time."

They gathered their weapons together then, for they always brought several different types – spears, staffs, halberds, knives and maces. But Asana was not quite done with the lesson. As they hurried back toward the underground halls to get out of the weather, he kept speaking.

"What you do now in sparring is as close as you can get to a real fight. But the gap is still large. Nothing can properly prepare you for that. Nothing. Fear surges. Your heart pounds. What you thought you knew, abandons you. Your confidence that was high becomes doubt instead. These things you should know, and accept. Think on it often, and it won't catch you by surprise when the storm of death is upon you."

It wasn't exactly encouraging, but Faran sensed the truth in the man's words.

"Is there a remedy for this beforehand? Some way to train for it that we're not yet doing?" Ferla asked.

"No, there's nothing. But you must grasp this. Sometimes to win a fight you must embrace death. Accept it. Make your peace with that thought. For only then can you conquer fear. Fear holds you back in a fight. It steals strength from mind and body. It makes you hesitate. By embracing death, you give yourself the best chance to live."

Faran happened to be looking closely at Asana as he spoke, and he noticed the man's eyes grow hard with determination.

16. Down the Mountain

The next day the weather had cleared. The sky was deep blue, without a single cloud, and it seemed as though it would stay that way.

Faran loved it, and he loved more that he and Ferla were heading on a journey with Kubodin. Several times a year the little man took his mule down the mountain and to a small village to buy supplies. Mostly, the garden atop the mountain was enough, but they could not grow everything they needed there, especially flour and grains. This was a good time to go, the little man had announced at dawn that morning, and he had invited them.

Asana did not object, and he said a break from training would do them good. It would help their bodies to heal from strains and allow overused muscles and ligaments a rest.

So it was that they walked beside Kubodin's mule as the sun rose and a cool, but not cold breeze blew. Kubodin rode, and he whistled and even sang little snatches of song in his native tongue as they went. It seemed that he was happy for the change of routine as well.

Faran and Ferla did not wear their armor, but had their swords of course. They went nowhere unprepared. The swords would make them stand out more, but that could not be helped. The danger was slight though, for warriors were common enough.

Kubodin had his axe, as usual. But his cheerful attitude was not normal. It seemed rather strange, but the little man was always unpredictable. Strange or otherwise though, Faran had grown to like him. Even his rough way of speaking. He was the opposite of Asana in nearly every way, but not the ways that mattered.

Winter was beginning to close in, and even at the thought of it Faran's heart went back to the valley of the lake and the good times they had enjoyed there. Winter had brought them all closer together, and though the cabin had been small they never grew tired of each other's company.

He had grown closer to Ferla there, too. But if the cabin was no more, and though they might never see the valley again, that closeness remained. And had strengthened.

There was something between them. But what? He was not so sure. She loved him, he knew. And he loved her. But did she still look upon him as a younger brother? He had seen no suggestion otherwise.

"What's the name of this village we're going to?" Ferla asked, interrupting Kubodin in the middle of him whistling a raspy tune.

"Hey? What was that?"

"What village are we going to?"

"Oh, that. I never pay much heed to names. Useless things for the most part. Why, even this mule, can you guess his name?"

They could not, and Kubodin told them. "His name is Mule," he said with a laugh as though it were a great joke. "See what I mean? Names don't do much. Unless they're elven names, of course. Those folks see to the heart of things, and they give names that stick because they're true."

There was silence for a little while after that. The only sound was the hooves of the mule on the steep slope where they clattered against an outcrop of rock.

Faran and Ferla walked with great care, for it was very steep here. Even at times they went to hands and knees to clamber down. But the mule looked at home, negotiating it all with ease. No horse could have done that, and Faran did recall being told once that a mule was far more surefooted in steep country. What appeared to be at first an eccentric choice by Kubodin was well-grounded in reality.

They came to a less steep path, and Kubodin looked back and grinned at them.

"Drummald Village, it's called. It can be a rough place, and Camar and Duthenor and even Cheng are there at times. Some of them are hiding, and it's a good place to do it. There's nothing all around but the flat lands and battle sites. And there's certainly no king. They rule themselves."

It sounded to Faran as though Kubodin approved of that last fact. He was not so sure himself. Druilgar had turned out to be a bad king. But a good one? Well, that was a different matter. A good king brought peace, the rule of just law and prosperity. Those were things to seek.

"Tell us about Asana?" Ferla asked.

Kubodin looked suddenly serious. "He's a great man. There are few like him. Very few."

His respect for Asana was obvious. They were friends, even though at first it seemed to Faran that they were master and servant. But one did not preclude the other. Yet still, he had told them nothing they did not already know. But he was not done. He seemed to guess their curiosity about a man who trained them, but kept his personal distance as he did so and spoke seldom about himself.

"He is half Cheng, as you know, and half Duthenor. But he's at home among neither people. He spent most of his youth among the Cheng, but he was bullied there. No one would teach him how to fight, but at length he met one master who recognized his inborn athleticism and determination to learn. And he learned, surpassing any student the master had ever had. In humility, which is rare among the Cheng masters, that master soon realized his student would outstrip him and recommended him to one of the great masters. After that, he was bullied no more. People became scared of him, and they showed reverence to him because of who his teacher was. But he never forgot being bullied, and it made him into a quiet man, which is not healthy."

Kubodin clamped his jaw shut, and said no more. Perhaps he thought he had said too much, for he nudged the mule into a trot and got ahead of them.

Towards the afternoon they reached the lower slopes of the mountain and then passed into flat lands. Mostly, it was grassland, but here and there small stands of trees grew. It was a place like neither Dromdruin nor the valley of the lake, and Faran did not really like all this open space.

But they did need supplies, and he was glad to come. A land that was new appealed to him, even if it was a place he would not wish to live.

As the long shadows of afternoon set in, they came to Drummald Village.

It was a ramshackle place. Some attempt at a village wall had been made, but the six-foot poles skewered into the ground, their tops sharpened to points, only circled about a third of the perimeter. Down the center ran a dirty track. Here, a few people stood and watched the newcomers. Piglets ran to and fro among them.

The village itself was larger than Faran would have guessed, and there was a strange mix of housing styles. Some were even a little grand, if dilapidated. Some had wide porches, others no porches and steep roofs. Many were little more than mud and wattle huts. It was a strange looking place.

But Kubodin, whistling softly, led them down the center of the track. He slowed though when some armed men appeared from a building nearby and approached.

Kubodin fingered his axe, and tension rose. "Hey! Is there a problem here?"

The armed men looked them over, their eyes lingering on their weapons.

"Not unless you make one," the leader replied. He was a tall fellow, older than the others and the surest of himself.

"Then why the big reception, huh?" Kubodin did not remove his hand from near his axe.

"They're all right," one of the men said from behind the leader. "That's Kubodin. He comes here a few times a year for supplies. Never seen the other two before."

The man who spoke looked a bit like Kubodin himself, but not as fierce. At any rate, the leader seemed relieved.

"Fair enough. Come into town then, and welcome. We have to be careful these days. There have been bandits from time to time."

Faran was a little surprised. He had these men, and the whole village, figured for a group of thieves hiding from the law. But it seemed that even thieves had thieves preying on them.

Kubodin nodded, and cast a grin at the man at the back who had spoken for him.

"You want to dice later?"

The man at the back grunted. "Not against you. You skinned me clean out last time. You have the luck of a devil."

"Hey! Don't spread that around," Kubodin said. "Otherwise no one will let me join their table."

"You'll do all right. There are, as usual, plenty of new folks in town who haven't lost money to you before."

Kubodin led them down the main street then. The shadows were getting long, but there was a kind of general store in the middle of the village that was still open. It was one of the biggest buildings, and was nothing like what Faran had seen before. There had never been shops in Dromdruin Village, but he had heard of them.

Kubodin hitched the mule to a post and went inside, and Faran and Ferla followed. The building was larger than it seemed, and they wandered around looking at things while Kubodin spoke with the shop owner. He ordered a great many things and arranged for them all to be ready to be picked up tomorrow morning.

Tonight, they would spend in one of the two inns. Faran was looking forward to this. It was an adventure for him, but Ferla seemed less inclined to agree. *Drunk men and beer breath*, she muttered when he had raised the subject, but Kubodin certainly seemed excited by the prospect and that lifted Faran's spirits.

"All done," Kubodin said when they were outside again. "Sadly, I'll have to walk back tomorrow. Mule here will be heavily burdened, but hey, at least I rode down the mountain."

It was not far to the inn that Kubodin apparently favored. They paid for the mule to be kept in the barn overnight and fed, then went inside.

Straight away, Faran knew that Ferla had been right not to like the idea of staying here overnight. There were people everywhere, and many of them were drunk. That was a sight seldom seen in Dromdruin, even at the midwinter festival. There was a lot of noise too, mostly men singing and laughing loudly.

Kubodin seemed to love it. His face lit up with glee, and he went to the bar and bought them all drinks. These

Faran and Ferla sipped, but Kubodin gulped his down and then belched. Faran began to understand why apparently Asana never joined the little man on this journey.

A group of people left, and a small table became free. This Kubodin was quick to claim, and at least they had a place to sit down in a corner that was somewhat quieter than near the bar itself.

Faran looked around, studying the place. Behind the bar and secured high up on the wall were the remains of some beast. It was only bones and a great set of tusks, but it was huge and something Faran had never seen before.

Kubodin must have seen him looking. "Dug up from one of the nearby battlefields," he said. "Who knows what it's called, but there are many such skeletons around. Creatures of the Shadow," he said, his voice dropping low.

Faran could believe it. The thing had a bad look to it, and he wondered how many men had died in battle to kill such a beast.

Looking around, he saw that there were many other objects on the walls. Rusted swords and shields predominated, but there were other weapons too that he had no name for. Some were far too large for a man to wield. But most were in poor condition and looked like they might break apart and fall at any moment.

Kubodin left them at the table, and he visited others where games of dice were being played. They watched him for a while, and it seemed he was enjoying himself immensely.

"He's going to get drunk," Ferla said.

It was probably true. He had been back to the bar several times, and drunk quite a bit already while they were still sipping their first drinks.

"I can see why Asana lives far from others," Faran answered. "Partly to keep Kubodin out of trouble, but also to avoid all this." He pointed with his finger to take in the whole room.

"I know what you mean. I'd rather just you and me and the top of the mountain. Or being back in the valley. Those were good times Faran, but our world has moved on."

He was surprised at that comment. Where did she see herself in the future? But it was a question without answer, for the both of them.

The evening passed. They ate a hearty stew for dinner, which Faran loved after only eating vegetables for months, and they sipped on a second round of beer.

Kubodin came back to them regularly, drunker each time than the last. But his pockets also rattled with the coin that he had won in dice and card games. He would talk for a little while, but then his eyes would get a gleam in them as he saw some new game start up and he would saunter off.

They had rooms upstairs, ready and paid for, but Faran and Ferla, though they did not really like it down here in the bawdy common room, did not want to miss the experience. It was so different from anything they were used to.

The evening wore on and it grew late. Most of the revelers had gone home, but here and there a game of dice was still going on and Kubodin, though swaying when he walked to the bar for yet more to drink, still seemed energetic.

It was then that some newcomers entered the bar. Faran saw them first, and he brought Ferla's attention to them.

There was something wrong. These men were not drunk. That alone made them stand out. There were ten of them, and some wore armor, though it looked poorly made. All, however, wore swords.

A hush fell over the common room, but before anyone could react or speak the ten men drew their swords. Two of them guarded the door, ensuring no one came in or left.

The leader was a squat man with an ugly face. Boils stood out from his skin, but his armor was the best and by the way he held his sword and moved Faran knew he was a skilled warrior.

"Do as you're told," the squat man said. "And you'll live. Now, give us your coins and valuables."

These were the bandits that they had been warned of when they entered the village, and Faran cursed his luck.

Neither he nor Ferla were drunk. But everyone else was, and though there were other men with swords in the room, Faran doubted that the ten bandits could be defeated. They had timed their robbery perfectly. The inn had emptied of most of its patrons, but the night's takings were still here.

Kubodin was not so close as Faran would have liked. He was halfway across the room. But as the bandits spread out, holding up bags for people to put their coins and jewelry into, one of them approached him and shook the bag.

"Your coins!" he commanded.

Kubodin looked him up and down. "And if I don't agree?"

"Then you're a dead man," the bandit hissed.

A silence fell over the room, and Kubodin answered loud enough for all to hear, suddenly not so drunk as he had appeared.

"I don't think so, pretty boy."

There was a moment's pause, and then the sudden speed of Kubodin shattered the stillness. Somehow a knife was in his hand, and he whipped it at the bandit's throat.

Crimson blood sprayed everywhere, but even as the man stood there clutching his neck in a futile attempt to stop the bleeding, Kubodin was moving on.

The knife was gone as quick as it appeared, and now the axe was in his hands. He leaped at another bandit and uproar broke out.

Faran's choice was made for him, and his indecision was gone. He stood and flung the table over, tripping a bandit close by. Then he darted to the side, sword drawn, and Ferla was with him.

Together they attacked the bandits who had moved on Kubodin. The little man stood with his back to the wall, his axe flashing and several dead men near him already.

The squat leader bellowed for his men to take him down, but Faran engaged him, his sword striking out in a deadly arc.

The squat leader was good. Faran sensed that straight away. Fear ran through him, and he backed away as the other man attacked, hewing at him with powerful but well-controlled blows.

But Faran blocked them. Steel rang against steel, and the greater fight that had broken out in the room was lost to him. His every thought was now on this life and death contest.

The bandit kept coming at him, but Faran found his rhythm. Soon, he no longer blocked the other man's blows but deflected them with grace.

The squat man slowed, and a look of surprise crossed his face. It was then that Faran attacked. He moved into Tempest Blows the Dust, his blade dizzyingly fast.

To this, the bandit had no answer and he retreated on surprisingly agile steps. Faran did not let up though. He pursued swiftly, and moved into Hawk Folds its Wings so as not to be predictable.

This downward thrust nearly killed his opponent. The man had not expected that, perhaps never even seen the move before. He was gifted, but not as skilled as Faran had taken him for.

Faran took a step back, and he moved into Cherry Blossom Falls from the Tree. This lowered his sword tip slightly, indicating tiredness. But it was a trap, and the squat man fell for it. He hastened in, raising his sword for an overhand strike, but Faran darted forward himself, the tip of his sword lifting and flitting through the air with a dark gleam.

The squat man's throat disappeared in a spray of blood, and he fell to the floor gurgling and twitching. Faran leaped over him and into the fray around Kubodin. He had no time to dwell on the fact that he had just killed a man.

Kubodin was hemmed in, his back to the wall. Discord, his twin-bladed axe flashed and a bandit's head toppled and bounced on the floor. To the left, Ferla engaged a tall and thin man. He swung a mighty blow at her, but deftly she deflected it.

Faran shouted and ran at the man, battle rage pounding through his body with every heartbeat. But before he got there, Ferla had opened a vein in the bandit's leg, another in his arm and even as the man tried to retreat the point of her sword slipped through his defenses, penetrated his poorly made mail shirt and forced its way up until it burst his heart.

Blood poured from the man's mouth. Ferla disengaged her blade by kicking him off it and pulling it back at the same time, a move he had watched her practice countless times but that was now surreal to see in real life. Her red hair flowed to one side, but a spray of blood marked her face.

Faran drew close. He saw another dead bandit near her, his head half hacked off. Ferla had been busy while he had dueled the squat man.

Together they attacked the remaining bandits that had backed Kubodin against the wall. They were not the first. Some of the patrons of the inn had joined in. They wielded swords, knives and even chairs. The barman laid about him too with a mighty cudgel.

But it was Kubodin that was the most ferocious of them all. Laughing as he fought, he plunged into his attackers and chaos ensued.

It was over in moments. Faran and Ferla each killed another man, and a pile of bodies lay at Kubodin's feet. He laughed again, and held his axe high shaking it vigorously. "Discord! You're as dangerous as ever!" he shouted.

Then he strode toward them, a grin splitting his face and blood dripping down his arm. It was not his own, but came from the axe.

"Hey! Now that was a good fight!" He turned to the barman. "But it was thirsty work! I need another drink!"

Faran and Ferla shared a room with two beds that night. Kubodin said money was tight, and he winked at them. He did not know that they had shared a room back in the cottage by the lake. There had never been any romance then, and there would not be now. They had killed men, and they felt the weight of that.

But they both knew also that the bandits had brought it on themselves. They would still be alive if they were not thieves threatening, and prepared to murder, innocent people if they did not hand over their money.

So they talked well into the night, whispering quietly of what had happened. This much at least they were glad to know. In a real fight, with their lives in jeopardy, their skills had not failed them. They also knew now the difference between sparring, however hard, and facing an enemy actually trying to kill them. That knowledge was invaluable. It could not be taught.

Eventually they slept, though they could hear Kubodin laughing in the room next door, and there seemed to be someone with him. They ignored that.

The next morning they gathered their stores from the shop and packed them securely on the mule. Faran felt sorry for it because it would be hard going uphill. But the three of them also strapped packs to their backs and bore some of the burden.

It was still early when they left, but there was a cheer from some of the villagers as they passed. The killing of the bandits made life safer for them.

Faran ventured the view that they had sent a signal to their true enemies. Their swords might be recognized as blades of Kingshield Knights, but Kubodin, quiet and subdued now by a hangover, did not think so. Few would ever recognize the swords for what they were, and skilled warriors and fights were commonplace.

Faran was not so sure.

17. The Shadow of Winter

The fight at the inn had a profound effect on the way Faran and Ferla sparred. They knew, now, the difference between reality and similitude, and their way of moving changed slightly as a result.

What had just been words to them before, spoken either by Aranloth or Asana, now suddenly became weighted with meaning. If the point of their sword was a handspan too low, it might be the difference between life and death, and they now knew the value of those little verbal corrections to their posture. Or in the case of Asana, more likely he just gave a visual cue, emphasizing something in his own posture as he demonstrated a move.

Asana had questioned them about the fight too, probing how they had felt and reacted. No detail was too small, and he urged them to think deeply on what had happened, and why, and what they might do differently next time.

This was part of his training. He made them think for themselves, and evaluate things from different angles. Any fight, he had instructed them, was an opportunity to learn. But not to berate themselves for mistakes made, just to incorporate the lessons into their practice.

It seemed good advice to Faran. But Asana showed another side too. He was clear that the way of the warrior was not to seek trouble needlessly, and to avoid battle. But only when possible. There would be times when trouble was brought to them, as it had been in the inn, and then they should learn to apportion guilt where it was due. And that was on the perpetrators of the violence. If they died, the guilt for that was theirs. If they were maimed, so too it was their fault.

Ferla especially needed to hear that, for Faran knew that she felt badly over what had happened. He had felt something of the kind himself. He knew he should not have, but somehow the feelings crept up on him anyway.

But Asana had set their minds at rest, and that he saw the need for such teaching, and that he cared enough to give it, was an indication that he had been in that situation himself, and that despite his cool exterior there was a bond between them.

Kubodin, when he had recovered from his hangover, merely laughed and reminded them that it had been a good fight, and that bad men had got what they deserved. He had also told them that likely they had saved lives, for those bandits had committed murder in the past and would have done so again. So he too, for all that his manner was rough, understood exactly how they felt and worked to ease their guilt.

Kareste left those lessons to Asana and Kubodin. But her eyes were deep wells of emotion, and Faran knew what she was thinking. There would be more fights and more death before this was over.

He knew she was right, so he trained even harder than he had before.

And what he faced just now atop the mountain was the hardest training he had ever endured. He and Ferla fought together, trying to fend off both Asana and Kubodin.

Asana wielded his thin sword with a quiet but deadly grace that was frightening. Kubodin came at them with his axe. He laughed as he hacked and hewed, but his attacks were very nearly as dangerous as Asana's.

But on top of that, Kareste also struck at them, mostly lashing out with magic but also striking deftly with her staff.

Swords clashed. Sparks flew. Faran and Ferla fought together, maneuvering so as to try to keep their backs to each other and protect themselves as best they could.

A streak of lòhrengai flashed at Ferla. Even as she summoned a shield of flame to protect herself, she also deflected a killing thrust from Asana.

Faran, his arms trembling from weariness for the sparring had been going on for quite some time, flung fire from his left hand at Kareste while the sword in his right thrust at Kubodin.

Kareste raised her own shield of flaring magic and blocked his assault with ease. But at least it prevented her from continuing her attack on Ferla. Kubodin likewise darted back out of harm's way, but even as he retreated his axe swept sideways in an attempt to knock Faran's sword from his hand.

This was a fight Faran could not win. He knew that, and so did Ferla. They were outnumbered, and their opponents surpassed them in skill. The result was inevitable.

But victory in this contest would not come by winning. It would come by enduring as long as they could against an assault that was beyond them. Endurance was a victory. Fighting together, back to back and forcing their opponents to fight them eye to eye, rather than a tap of the sword on their backs was a victory. The confidence gained by holding their own, even just for a time, against such an onslaught was the greatest victory of them all.

Faran was not fast enough to withdraw his sword and avoid Kubodin's blow, so instead he used the flat of the blade to resist the strike with force. But that was a ploy.

Kubodin continued the strike, trying to dislodge the weapon, and in doing so he overcommitted and leaned too far forward. Suddenly Faran used his wrist to roll the blade out from underneath the axe and at the same time kicked with his left leg at Kubodin's knee. It was a strike intended to buckle the leg that supported all of Kubodin's weight.

Kubodin, always unpredictable, did the last thing Faran expected. He charged forward so that Faran's leg strike missed, and with his shoulder he rammed into Faran's chest.

Faran sprawled backward. His sword spun from his grip, but even as he tried to rise Kubodin rushed him and Kareste sent a spurt of lòhren-fire toward him.

He rolled and grasped his sword, but he knew his battle was over. Yet even as he thought that a wild idea occurred to him.

Acting on instinct alone he summoned magic, and he did what he had seen Aranloth do. He formed the image of a warrior, only that warrior was himself. Then weaving a shield around the image he fended off Kareste's attack and slipped away in conjured dust and smoke.

Kubodin struck at the image, but he seemed perplexed. Kareste was not fooled though. She had seen what Faran had done, but she was surprised. He managed to fling fire at her from one hand, and it struck her in the chest.

Even as they sparred with full intent, but withheld power from their blows, so it was with magic. The fire was little more than light only, but it still caused the edges of her cloak to smolder.

Suddenly Kubodin roared with laughter. "A pretty trick!" he cried. "But I see you now!"

The image Faran had summoned dissipated at Kubodin's blow. At the same moment, Kareste raised her staff but then slowly lowered it and stepped back. She had been defeated, and Faran's heart thudded. He had never done that before.

He turned to face Kubodin, but instead saw both the little man and Asana spread out to attack him. Ferla was to the side, and stepping away. Asana must have beaten her.

Faran tried to move to the side so as to keep Asana between him and Kubodin, but the little man was too nimble and darted around and attacked even as did Asana.

Deftly jumping back, Faran deflected a thrust from Asana's blade, but even as he did so he felt the ring of a blow to his helm. Kubodin had struck the top of his head with the axe, and the sparring session was over.

They gathered together, as they usually did after a sparring session like this, and talked about it.

Kareste was the first to speak, and there was an element of surprise in her voice.

"How did you do that, Faran? Even I struggle to create images of people like that."

"I don't know. It just happened. I guess I saw Aranloth do it a lot, and somehow I caught the knack for it."

Kareste frowned. "It's more than a knack. You have great talent in that direction."

"But I would still have split his skull with my axe," Kubodin said, and he grinned wickedly.

"You both did well," Asana said. "Neither I nor Kubodin are easy to spar against. And over and above that, you held Kareste at bay for a good while as well. Everything was against you, but you still performed." He offered them a small bow then, a thing he rarely did.

Faran was exhausted, and he saw that Ferla was too. But they grinned at each other. A bow from Asana was high praise indeed.

They spoke for a while after that, but the weather atop the mountain turned swiftly as it often did. The sky was only partly filled with clouds, yet out of them a sprinkling of snow began to fall. It was the first of the season, and winter was upon them.

Tired, but happy, they went inside for shelter against the cold, and Faran was pleased with the change in the weather. It would make it harder for their enemies to search them out, but he did wonder what steps they were taking to do so.

18. The King's Favor

Savanest meditated, alone, in his tent and before a small but hot fire set within a brazier. His camp, and his company of soldiers, was established on the escarpment that overlooked the land known as the Angle. It was the heartland of the Letharn empire of old, and Aranloth had come here.

Here also, he had disappeared. Savanest knew how that was done.

The lòhren had ventured into the tombs. It was a deed that few would attempt. But Aranloth had courage, and he possessed some means of doing so safely. Whatever that means was, it was a secret. For anyone else, entering the tombs was death. So the tales told, and Savanest believed them. He had stood at the entrance, and there he had sensed a great magic hidden within. The malice of it had buffeted him like a wind, though the soldiers with him had sensed little.

He had nearly sent some in to test the nature of that magic, but there had been no point. The end result was certain. Death. Nor did he wish to kill men needlessly, for they might be needed later. Most of all, it would not help him find the seventh knight.

Aranloth had entered the tombs with those he protected, and from one of the exits, and no doubt there were many, he had escaped undetected. Worse, the seventh knight would have obtained a weapon and armor in there. This was where Aranloth obtained them. It was not widely known among the knights that this was so, but there were records, and Savanest had read them long ago.

It was only when he had come here though that the memory returned to him. That was a pity because it would have been a chance to set a trap.

It should have been over now though. But Lindercroft had failed. By a stroke of luck, he had discovered where their enemies had hidden in a remote valley. He had surrounded them in a cottage and attacked, but despite his soldiers and his own skill with blade and sorcery, the seventh knight had escaped.

Only one thing mattered now. The seventh knight must be found and killed. To let him live was to provide a rallying point for all the forces that might oppose the rule of the king and the knights. The prophecy must be quashed. Hope extinguished. Only then would the populace be willing to look at the new order of the world and embrace it. They must be given no other choice.

Savanest considered what to do next. His brother knight, Sofanil, had also set out on the hunt. Three knights now searched out the enemies of the kingdom, and it was typical of the king that it should be so. He set them against each other. Perhaps this was to find the strongest and ablest among them to help shoulder the burden of rulership in the great days to come. Or maybe it was a plot to keep them vying against each other so that no one would have time to think of supplanting him.

But it did not matter either way. Regardless, Savanest intended to rise above the other knights and assume a greater role than they.

Yet he was in doubt. Where to search for the enemy? To that end, Lindercroft was best placed to help him. Not that he would deliberately, but by speaking to him it might be possible to learn some of what he concealed. He must know, or guess, something.

So it was that Savanest began the rite. He performed it as the king had instructed him, focusing his mind on

Osahka, thinking only of the stone and drawing a knife across his palm to provide blood. This was the catalyst of the magic, and it was a small and near-painless sacrifice compared to the power of magic obtained.

His blood sizzled momentarily as air, fire and the red fluid itself combined in puffs of dark smoke. Then he uttered the words of power just as he had been taught. Sudden pain ripped through his palm, and afar in the Tower of the Stone he felt the thought of Osahka leap out to him.

The twining tendrils of flame flared, and within their moving filaments an image grew and took shape.

"What do you wish?" came the crackling voice of Lindercroft. He did not seem best pleased, but the king had commanded them to cooperate, so he could not refuse to talk.

"Greetings, Knight Lindercroft," Savanest said. No matter the rivalry between them, it need not show. "I seek word of your progress."

Lindercroft frowned, though it was hard to tell in the flickering image of flame. Similarly, his voice sounded like the burning timber. Savanest was not accustomed to this type of magic, and he was not the most skilled at it. A fact that had earned him sly grins from the others. But he would repay that insult. At least, when the time was right.

"I seek the enemy still," Lindercroft replied. "They cannot remain hidden forever."

Savanest gritted his teeth. That was an answer which told him nothing.

"Where are you focusing your search?"

Lindercroft hesitated. This was information he could not withhold, but he still considered his answer carefully.

"My forces are divided, but for the most part they search the area north of the valley where the boy was last seen."

Savanest allowed himself a smile. Their quarry was more than a boy. He had, after all, eluded Lindercroft multiple times. That was an embarrassment, and Lindercroft knew what he was thinking for his frown deepened.

That was of no concern. They were supposed to cooperate with each other, but Lindercroft had left things as vague as possible by saying that his forces were divided.

No doubt his searchers were dispersed, but it left him plausible deniability if he were accused of not passing information on. He would be working on a theory, but he would also be casting as wide a net as possible in case his theory was wrong. The elù-draks were of great assistance in that regard, for they could survey enormous amounts of territory.

Should the comment that he searched especially north of the valley where the enemy had last been seen be given weight? It was not far from where Savanest was now. That was convenient. Too convenient. It suggested Lindercroft did not want him to move. Likewise, if he said he was searching north of the valley, likely he was trying to hide the area of his deepest suspicion. That might well be the opposite direction.

"Have you given thought," Savanest continued, "that they would head northward to the city of Cardoroth? That is a place well-suited to hiding and where the lòhrens have many contacts."

Lindercroft seemed surprised at that. "It could be. It's a long way to travel, but as you say it would be nearly impossible for anyone to find them there. Yes, that's a very real possibility."

Savanest did not trust this man, least of all now. His surprise had not been genuine. He would have been a fool not to consider the possibility, and this was more confirmation that his true area of search was to the south and not the north.

It was time to change the subject. Savanest would learn no more on this one, and if he pressed it Lindercroft would realize he had not been believed. Better to keep him in doubt about that. Otherwise, he would be on his guard and take more active measures to conceal his activities.

"There is unrest in Faladir," Savanest stated. This was dangerous ground, for it could be seen as a criticism of the king. But it would also distract Lindercroft from their previous conversation and lull him into the thought that he had been believed.

Lindercroft sneered. He had changed over the years, and the expression seemed strange on his face.

"There are always those who cannot see the right way forward, even if that path is before their feet."

"That is true," Savanest replied. "Yet it is disturbing, and though the unrest is rarely spoken, it seethes beneath the surface."

Lindercroft considered that. The sneer was gone now, and he looked as he had when they first met, which was intelligent and thoughtful. Savanest could not help but wonder how he had changed himself, but he schooled his thoughts away from that. He always did lately. Aranloth had encouraged introspection, but Aranloth was Osahka no more, and introspection was troubling…

"Do you truly see a danger in this?" Lindercroft asked.

"I do. The populace is like the forest after several years of drought. It is quiet now, but one spark and it could erupt in flame."

Lindercroft shrugged. "It may be so, but it is up to us to make sure there is no spark."

He did not seem worried. In truth, there was little reason to be. Yet still a doubt nagged at Savanest. It should have been easy to kill a young man and his companions, but so far they had not been able to do so. Was it really fated that there would be a seventh knight? Was Aranloth's prophecy more than just legend?

"You have met this young man who is supposed to be a threat. What is he like?"

"I know little of him. Faran, he is called. He has courage, which I'll not deny. But he is an untutored, uncultured farm boy of no account. He is not a knight, nor ever will be."

Savanest heard an undertone in those words. There was frustration and animosity there. For all that Lindercroft was a smart and discerning man, he might be blinded by that. The so-called farm boy had bested him more than once, and if ever anything blinded someone to the truth it was enraged pride.

"What of the girl with him from Dromdruin Village?"

"Her?" Lindercroft's sneer returned. "She is nothing. She is a nobody caught up in events beyond her control and understanding. She is of no account."

Savanest felt uneasy. Lindercroft dismissed them all, but there was something disturbing about them. Yet still, he had met them both, so perhaps his word should be taken on these things.

"Then I will leave you, Knight Lindercroft. There are no further issues to discuss."

The sneer on Lindercroft's face grew. He knew that this magic was difficult for some of the knights. Savanest resented that, for he was superior in many other ways, but he felt a pain growing behind his eyes, which was a sure sign he had overtaxed himself with magic.

Lindercroft bowed, more to hide his expression than out of courtesy, and Savanest released the magic. There was a sudden puff of smoke, and the fire in the brazier went out. Touching it, the metal was cold.

Savanest shivered. He still felt a sense of unease. Perhaps it was because his brother knight, Sofanil, had also joined the search. He would like to know what he was doing, but that would have to wait until tomorrow. He was too tired now to invoke the magic a second time.

But doubt was an enemy, and he cast it from his mind. Whoever killed the seventh knight would be raised above all others, and Savanest knew it would be him. He felt it to his very bones. He even sensed the Morleth Stone whisper it in his mind. But that too was a problem. He had been gone from the stone too long, and he yearned to return to its presence.

The sooner he killed Faran, the sooner that would be.

19. The Training of a Sage

The winter wind howled outside. But in the main hall of Danath Elbar, although they could hear it moan in the tunnel, it remained warm despite the stone surroundings.

Fires burned in several hearths, and cunningly concealed flutes in the stone channeled away smoke. That smoke, Kubodin had told Faran, was dispersed at several points atop the mountain. It would not create a single plume that might attract the eyes of any wanderers in the wild. This was good, because the only wanderers in the current weather would likely be searching for them and be servants of Lindercroft.

They rarely trained outside now, which was a thing that Asana did not like. Better to train in the fresh air he had told them, and in the morning. The world was full of life then, and it was healthy for the body.

But the cold had forced them inside. At least mostly. Asana still took them out for brief periods, especially in the snow. He wanted them to get used to fighting on all sorts of terrain and in all sorts of weather. A warrior had to be well rounded and experienced, he repeated to them many times. It was no good just being able to execute pretty patterns on level grass. Battle was often not like that. You could be caught on a narrow mountain trail fighting bandits. Or in the snow. Or fording a creek. A true warrior trained for all eventualities.

It was after lunch now though, and they had put aside their weapons for the day. What they trained now was intended instead to sharpen their wits, and to improve their minds.

Aranloth had trained them this way too, his discourses covering history, negotiation, poetry and all manner of things.

But Asana had used that foundation and taken them deeper into several topics. He seemed to enjoy this even more than the weapons training. He had told them, on any number of occasions, that in his land a true warrior was also a sage – a man of wisdom and learning, and that the mind was a sharper weapon than any sword.

Faran understood enough now to know it was true. Knowing when to fight was just as important as doing so successfully. Words could win battles. Or lose them. A leader needed more than a sword to inspire followers.

Despite the fluted stone that removed the smoke, the scent of it was still in the room. Faran liked it, and he liked also that for these conversations everyone was present.

Kubodin rarely spoke, but he was always there. Now, he sat on a rug on the floor beside Asana, his axe cradled in his lap while he endlessly ran a whetting stone over the blades. He grinned as he did so. Kareste was on the other side of Asana, in a chair, her staff laid down on the floor beside her and her green-brown eyes fixed on the strange man who was both weapons master and sage.

There had been a pause in the conversation, but now Asana spoke again.

"What is the nature of beauty?"

Faran glanced at Ferla, then answered quickly. "Beauty makes the heart beat faster, and quickens the breath. It makes you feel glad to be alive, and that all is right with the world. It's not a thing in itself, but an influence on people. That's why beauty is different things to different people."

Kubodin looked up from where he sharpened the axe blades, and the whetstone slowed, but he did not speak. Asana nodded.

It was Kareste who asked the next question. She and Asana often took turns at this.

"Ferla. What is evil? Is the hawk that hunts and kills the dove a creature of the shadow?"

Faran knew what he believed, but he wanted to know what Ferla's view was. But she did not answer straight away. She sat still, a slight frown on her face and her head tilted just barely to one side as she thought. It was a typical expression of hers.

"Nothing in nature," she said at last, "is either good or evil. It just is. The hawk is no more evil than a cold wind that blows from the north and kills lambs in winter. Nor a dove more peaceful than the shade of a tree on a hot day. It is humanity, and the other sentient creatures of Alithoras, that have the capacity for good or evil. This is because they have choice. Without choice, there is just nature. With choice, good and evil evolve."

Asana studied her. "Do you really think then that freedom of choice is the origin of evil?"

"And also of good." She held the master's gaze.

Asana gave a curt nod of approval. His question had seemed to indicate he did not agree with her answer, but he often acted so in order to put pressure on them to see if they would bend their beliefs under duress. At least, that was why Faran thought he did it.

The penetrating gaze of the master turned on him. Those eyes seemed remote, but Faran had caught glimpses of deep emotion behind them. Asana's expression was a protective mask, as much as a helm was armor. Kubodin had once said that the man had been bullied as a youth. It had marked him, making him wary and distrustful of showing his feelings.

"What," the master asked, "is the purpose of the universe?"

It was a big question, and the Faran that had been a simple hunter in Dromdruin Valley would have struggled to find an answer. But Aranloth had changed him, and he replied at once and with confidence.

"That's a flawed question, for it seeks to impose a stricture on the answer and deny a free response."

Asana raised an eyebrow, but he did not look displeased.

"How so?"

"The question supposes as a fact that the universe was created. Only a *created* universe can have a purpose. A universe that grew from chaos into order by random chance has no purpose. It just is."

"But nothing comes from nothing. And isn't it the state of nature that order gives way to chaos rather than rising from it?"

Faran thought on that. "Again, the framing of your statement tries to direct my answer. You say that nothing comes from nothing, yet if the universe was not created then indeed all that we know came from nothing. Likewise, the cycles of nature are from one extreme to the other. Chaos leads to order. Order leads to chaos. They are faces of the same coin and need no creator."

Asana sat back in his chair. "Do you deny then that there *is* a creator?"

"I don't deny it. Nor do I see any evidence to support it. There are various nations spread all over Alithoras. Some believe in a single creator. Others in many. Some believe the universe really is random chance. Who is right? Who is wrong? That's a matter for their personal faith and no man can say they have no right to their beliefs, whatever they are. But as to the purpose of the universe, the better question is this. What purpose does humanity give itself? What do we strive for? Surely, even if we are created, we have the freedom to choose that ourselves.

Otherwise we are not alive but merely objects. Does the blacksmith's hammer have a purpose? Does it have a choice? No. The blacksmith uses it as he will. The hammer is merely metal and wood. It has no choice or purpose. To be alive is to choose, and in the choosing we show our purpose."

The wind howled, and the scent of smoke in the air grew strong as it was momentarily forced backward by some eddy in the air currents outside. Asana's dark eyes glittered, but again he did not look displeased.

It was Kareste who asked the next question. "Have either of you yet worked out the secret of the knights?"

Faran looked at Ferla. He saw in her gaze that she had no answer, and neither did he. It seemed to him that he had no way of knowing the answer, yet if that were so why did she ask the question?

"We don't know," Ferla answered.

"It will come to you, one day," Kareste answered. "It comes to all the knights, eventually."

Kareste had spoken softly, and there was some meaning in her words that Faran was trying to fathom, but Kubodin stopped sharpening his axe blades and grunted.

"This is all horse dung. Every one of you thinks too much. You can't *think* your way through life – that's not how it works." The little man drew himself up, the axe forgotten. "What more is there to life than this? Eat when you're hungry. Drink when you're thirsty. Feel your heart pound when a girl you like smiles at you. And put a knife in the belly of those who wish you harm! That's all the philosophy you need, and everything else is just a game of shadows played in your mind."

The little man slumped after that and went back to sharpening his axe. Faran glanced at Asana. If ever two men were more different, he had never met them. Yet a smile hovered over the master's face, and it was not condescending. There was a deep friendship here between these two despite their differences. Perhaps because of them.

20. Captured

Menendil sat on the bench near the entrance to The Bouncing Stone. He liked it there, especially of a winter's morning when the early sun warmed his aging bones and felt like a balm to his skin.

This was one such morning. He was drowsy too, for there had been noise during the night. Wild yells and galloping horses and the rattle of a fast-drawn carriage had woken him from sleep, and he had not rested well after that.

Something had happened. But what? The street was a good place to learn. The inn was not yet open, but if the right passerby came near he might learn something of interest. So far, he had seen only strangers, and those that he did know he did not trust. So he sat and enjoyed the sun, whiling away a bit of time.

The inn was ready to open, and it was cleaned inside from yesterday's customers and food was cooking. He could see the plume of smoke rise from the chimney at the back of the building, towering high before some tiny movement of air bent it like a broken tree in his direction.

He had almost gone to sleep when he felt a shadow pass in front of the sun. He jerked his head up, his hand going to the hilt of the knife concealed beneath his cloak.

"Easy, Mender," a voice said calmingly.

It belonged to a young man, and Menendil recognized him by his voice alone. He was still hard to see, for the sun was behind him.

"You startled me, Balan."

The young man sat down on the bench next to him. "Folks startle easy these days."

That was certainly true. Menendil sat back on the bench and rejoiced in the warm sunlight. Balan was exactly the sort of man he hoped to meet this morning. He was young, but softly spoken and not given to outbursts. He was as steady as an oak, despite his youth. And he was a patriot. All of which were good reasons why he was a member of the Hundred. In addition, he was in the army, and heard, from time to time, rumors of the king's plans.

"What was last night's commotion about?" Menendil asked.

Balan rubbed his hands together for warmth. While he did so, he glanced up and down the street to ensure no one was close enough to hear anything they said.

"It was a bad business. Rumor is, and I heard this from a friend who was involved, that they at last captured Caludreth."

Menendil stifled a groan. This was bad. Very bad indeed. So far as was known, Caludreth was the last knight alive, other than the current six. Not that he was a knight anymore, having been cast unfairly out of the order by the king.

"Apparently, he was the leader of a group of rebels."

"Aye. They call him Lord Greenwood, for he had become a forest bandit. At least, the king's law calls them bandits, but many of those outlaws are just and true men, cast out as was their lord from a land they were loyal to."

"Was he really a threat?" Balan asked. "The king spent much gold and many resources to capture him. It's said he was betrayed by one of his own."

That might be true. But Menendil was not so sure. It was the sort of lie the king would spread to encourage distrust among his enemies. If they dared not cooperate with each other, how could they unify to threaten him?

"I don't think he was a threat. Not as Lord Greenwood, anyway. He and his men kept to the forest, I hear, and they're strong there. But out in the open, they would fall swiftly before a small regiment." Menendil closed his eyes and sighed. "But as Caludreth, last knight alive who has not fallen to the shadow, who can say. He could have rallied many men if he came to Faladir."

Balan smiled ruefully. "Well, he has come to Faladir now. But he'll rally no men in chains. Even if he could speak. But I'm told he was badly beaten after the capture. He was unconscious most of the way back, his eyes swollen shut and his face blackened by many blows."

Menendil no longer felt the warmth of the sun. Inside him, a hot rage boiled to the surface, but he held it in check.

"That's no way to treat a man. Prisoner or otherwise. Yet they haven't killed him yet, and there's hope in that."

Balan glanced at him, his eyes narrowing. "Do you intend to try some rescue attempt?"

The fury in Menendil turned suddenly cold with fear. To attempt a rescue was folly.

"It's something to think on. Imagine what we could do if we had one such as Caludreth among us?"

He could not believe he had said those words, especially calmly.

Balan looked away. "You had better think fast then."

"Why?"

"Because for now, he's close to us. He's held in the barracks just down the road."

Menendil knew what the other man meant. It had nothing to do really with Caludreth being held close to them.

"You think they'll take him to the tower?"

Balan nodded. "Tonight, I hear. And in the Tower of the Stone, in the presence of evil, it's said a man can be turned to the shadow. The rumor I hear is that it's been done before."

Menendil had heard the stories too. There might be truth in them, or there might not. Stories ran wild in the streets, these days. But the man had not been executed yet. Better for the king to have killed him out in the wild lands than take him prisoner. Executing one such as he was a two-edged sword. It could quell unrest in the populace by fear. Or it could rouse them into action. But if he were to be executed, he would have been taken to the gaol in the palace. Taking him to the barracks near the tower was suggestive.

The decision was made before Menendil knew it, welling up from deep inside him.

"Caludreth was once a knight. Who knows? He may be so again. We have to save him, or at least make the attempt. He is the last alive of a once-great order, at least the last alive that has not turned to the shadow. We *must* help him, and all the more so because the royal bloodline is now gone."

The sun was rising higher and the street was getting busier.

"You would make him king?" Balan asked.

"If we win this struggle, then we'll have need of one. Who better than someone trained in the old ways of the knights?"

Balan did not answer. An old man hobbled down the street before them, his eyes wary and his head swiveling from side to side looking for potential threats. There were many such in the city lately, and not all walked on two legs.

When the old man had passed, Balan spoke. "You think big thoughts, Mender."

"Someone has to think them."

"And someone has to act them out."

"That's the hard part," Menendil agreed. "And the dangerous part. But isn't that why the Hundred was formed?"

Balan did not reply to that directly, but Menendil could read in his clear gaze and the set of his jaw that he agreed.

"Tonight isn't so far away. Once Caludreth is brought to the presence of the stone atop the tower, it may be too late. That leaves very little time to plan and think."

It also left less time for fear and better sense to change his mind, Menendil knew, and less still for the Hundred.

"Spread the word," Menendil instructed him. "I'll pass it on to all I can as well. Even though there's so little time left, we should still be able to gather most of them. Tell them to meet at noon in the warehouse of the wool merchant Nadrak. The side door will be open, but no one will be there. And tell them to come hooded. Best to keep our identities hidden."

"Is Nadrak one of us?"

"No. That's why we'll meet there."

Balan smiled grimly. "You could bring destruction down on his head if we're caught."

"That may be, but better him than one of our own. He's known to be a king's man, so he should be safe. If not, he won't get anything he doesn't deserve."

Balan sighed. "You're a harder man than you look, Mender. But I'll spread the word."

Balan left after that, walking away down the street with sure strides. Menendil wished he could be so confident himself.

But he could not. He was pitting himself, and the lives of others, against the might of evil. But it had to be done.

He got up and went inside the inn. He moved slowly though, feeling suddenly old and wearied not just in body but in spirit. Could a man really be turned to the shadow? What of free will?

He did not wish to know the answer. But if Caludreth were not rescued, he would find out.

21. Death and Magic

Menendil waited in the shadows of an alley. He had been here for quite some time, and fear built as the night wore on and nothing happened.

They had not expected Caludreth to be taken from the barracks to the tower early in the evening, but it was now approaching midnight and still there had been no sign of anything.

The few men with him were anxious too. The alley stank of fear, but that was in his mind rather than anything he smelled. No doubt, it would be the same for the other men spread out in other alleys, loitering on corners or discretely gathered a block away.

They all waited the sounding of his horn to act. But what if their information had been wrong and Caludreth was not going to be taken to the tower? Worse, what if the Hundred had been betrayed and even now the king's soldiers were closing in on them?

He took a step forward, coming to the mouth of the alley but hugging close to the deep shadows so he could not be seen. The Tower of the Stone hulked to his left, a massive structure, sinister looking in the darkness. It was the pride of the city, for it was a memorial of a great victory in a previous age. But inside was evil, and that was unsettling.

Across the road, and a little to his right were the barracks. There was no sign of activity there. No more than normal, anyway. There were always lights in some of the windows, and always at the front of the building too.

But nothing was happening tonight that was different from any other night.

He stepped back a pace, but still maintained his vigil. Something had to happen soon, or the nerves of the men would grow too great. Worse, if nothing happened at all on their first venture, his leadership would fall in doubt. The men needed a victory to bind them to him and to each other. If their first venture was a failure, why should they follow his lead in the future?

But they had followed him easily enough when they met this afternoon. He had been shocked how easy it was to talk them into this action. How easy it was to ask them to risk their lives. The guilt of that hung over him, and if anyone died tonight it would be his fault.

His wife had looked at him with steady eyes when he told her. For all that she had warned him of the many risks he took, both for his own life and for hers, she had merely nodded.

"It must be done," she agreed. "A Kingshield Knight shouldn't be executed. Or worse. Evil cannot go unchallenged."

That was all she had said, but after, when he had belted on his sword and pulled up his hood as evening fell, she had hugged him fiercely before he slipped out the back door and into the shadows.

She was at the inn now. She and the staff would have shut already, and the staff at least would think he had gone to visit a sick friend.

His thoughts drifted back to the meeting with the men. Huddled in a dark warehouse, sentries guarding the entrance, they had agreed to act at his suggestion and then agreed to his plan.

Guilt washed over him again, but then it was gone in a heartbeat. Like the soldier he had been in his youth, the needs of the present outweighed all else, and nothing now mattered but the task at hand.

Across the road, there was movement in front of the barracks. Torches flared. The large doors opened and men in armor spilled out and milled around.

Laughter drifted to him, but those soldiers looked nervous.

"Be ready," Menendil hissed quietly to the few men with him.

The horn he carried, strung by a leather cord around his waist, he freed and held before him. His hands trembled, but in the dark only he knew that.

More men came from the barracks. There was no sign of the king, which was just as well. He might already be in the tower. But there was a Kingshield Knight there, his silver armor gleaming in the light from many torches, and he stood tall and proud and aloof from the others. He was quiet where they joked and laughed. He was still where they moved about nervously.

Then two men came through the doors, and they were fierce looking warriors. Between them, they supported a third man. He was shackled, and it seemed that he could not walk without aid.

This was the moment. It had come at last. It could be no one else but Caludreth, and in the short space between barracks and tower was the time to strike. Once he was inside, there would be no saving him.

Menendil waited. If he blew the horn too soon, the captive could be taken back to the barracks. If he waited too late, the tower would be within reach.

The tension mounted. The Kingshield Knight strode forward, and the company of men, at least fifty strong, came with him. In their midst, Caludreth staggered forward between his two guards.

Time took forever to pass. The Kingshield Knight looked invulnerable, and the full weight of what the Hundred was about to attempt ground down on Menendil. Should he blow the horn? *Could* he blow the horn?

Caludreth staggered again. One of his guards slapped him across the face, and then hauled him forward. The soldiers around them jeered.

The sound of the horn shattered the night, and the sweet music of it filled the street and rolled out over the city.

Menendil forgot doubt and fear. He lowered the horn from his mouth and drew his sword, racing forward. All that lay before him now was the enemy, and the prospect of bringing justice.

His boots thudded against the cobbles. Behind him his men came on in a great rush. The soldiers seemed dumbfounded, and they hesitated. The knight was the first to react, drawing his great sword, and then his men followed suit.

The soldiers began to tighten their ranks, and they looked at Menendil and his men. But that was a mistake. Menendil came to a sudden halt before he reached the enemy. Pouring into the main street from other alleys, both behind the soldiers and in front of them, came the rest of the Hundred. Among them were bowmen who plied their trade.

Arrows hissed in the dark. Soldiers fell, screaming. Blood pooled over the cobbles, and the king's men, unprepared for an attack such as this, withered before the onslaught.

This was a moment of great danger. A single stray arrow could kill the man they had come to save. Or the Kingshield Knight could slay him, preferring Caludreth to be killed rather than rescued.

More arrows hissed. More men fell. Menendil could not believe his luck, for he had expected a quicker reaction than this. But he had timed it well, and the enemy were caught precisely between their two points of safety and could not decide whether to press ahead or retreat.

The indecision did not last. The Kingshield Knight cried out, his voice ringing with command.

"Close ranks! March to the tower!"

Menendil blew his horn again, and began to move.

The second blowing of the horn signaled it was time to cease the arrow storm. Now, men must fight face to face and blade to blade.

He leaped in, slashing at the nearest soldier. His sword skills were rusty, and the man blocked it easily enough. But he did not anticipate the riposte that slashed his neck and killed him.

All around, the clang of blades sounded. Menendil had few men with him, and they barely slowed the marching soldiers. But soon others of the Hundred reached them, blocking them from the front and harassing them from the rear. Only on Menendil's side was a weak point, but heading this way did not lead to safety.

The Kingshield Knight pressed on, and men fell before his sword. But the soldiers slowed, and some of them looked back. They knew they were surrounded, and that this was a fight they may not win. But they had comrades by the hundreds in the barracks nearby.

Yet Menendil had thought of that, too. His plan had been thought out quickly, but his old training had never been forgotten.

Some of his men splashed oil at the front of the barracks and set it alight. The archers peeled away from the fight and grouped themselves across the street from the great doors. There they stood and loosed arrows at any from within. This would prevent reinforcements coming out, but only for a time. There were other exits from the building, and in a short while the soldiers inside would rally, armor themselves, gather shields, and strike at their attackers.

The archers could not stand against that. But they did not have to. They, and the fire, merely needed to create confusion and buy a little time.

The soldiers came to a standstill, hemmed in, and at least for the moment, outnumbered. Now, the true fighting began. Menendil's men pushed hard, but many were not soldiers. Against that, the enemy was caught completely by surprise, and the flames leaping up at the front of the barracks must have filled them with fear. They had no way of knowing how large the force was that attacked them, and if more enemies would pour out of the alleys to spill their blood.

Men fell on both sides. The Kingshield Knight roared and cursed. He stepped back from the fray, his deadly sword lowering in his right hand. But that did not mean he had withdrawn from the battle. It was just the opposite.

A chill filled the air, and green flame, wicked and sickly, sprang to the knight's left hand. With a flicking motion like a man dislodging water from his hand that flame scattered ahead of him and into the Hundred that attacked from that side.

Some of the men went down, their cloaks burning like a torch and the skin and flesh beneath melting away. Other men dropped their swords and ran. They had been prepared to fight blade to blade, but they could not defy magic.

Menendil did not blame the men who ran. All around him he felt the fear of the Hundred, and their uncertainty. They might be next.

The attack faltered. The knight swung around, pushing a soldier out of his way and faced toward Menendil. The green fire flared again, and he raised his hand.

But at that moment Caludreth flung off the soldiers who held him. Raising his manacled hands, smoke swirled around him, turning, twisting, and then it shot out at the Kingshield Knight and enveloped him.

One of the Hundred, closest to the knight, threw a knife at him also, and the sound of it striking the silver helm was loud even above the battle din.

The green fire scattered as the knight lost control of the magic. But some of it burned Menendil's men, yet also some of it burned the knight's own soldiers.

Screams broke out, tearing the air as men burned alive. But the Hundred were angry now, and their moment had arrived. This was their chance, and they surged at the knight to prevent him from having a chance to gather himself and unleash more magic.

Menendil saw his chance too. He killed a soldier, and drove in toward the two guards of Caludreth. There was smoke all about them, and they seemed to have trouble seeing. Menendil used that, felling one while another comrade who had been close to him fought the other guard.

"Caludreth!" Menendil cried. "Freedom lies this way!"

Out of the swirling smoke the figure of Caludreth emerged. He staggered, and Menendil swapped his sword to his left hand and with his right arm supported the once-knight.

Some of the Hundred gathered round, fending off the soldiers who rallied and tried to prevent the escape. More smoke rose, seemingly to bubble up from the cobbles, and Menendil was away. They burst from the fray, and into clearer air.

By the flickering light of flame Menendil saw the face of the man he was trying to save. It was gray with weariness, bruised and caked with dried blood. One eye was swollen shut, but the other looked out fiercely. Here was a man who would fight until the very end, but that end was close unless he escaped now.

It was hard to tell friend from foe, but the Hundred had wrapped white bands around their right arms to distinguish themselves, and he fell into a group of them now. They gathered around him and helped support Caludreth while they staggered away.

They moved some way down the street, away from the tower. There several men waited. One held the reins of a horse, and another had a hammer in his hand.

"To the ground, my lord!" Menendil called. "This man will free you from your shackles."

Menendil had guessed that Caludreth would be restrained, and he had arranged both horse and blacksmith. He knew who the man was, but the others did not. He could be any blacksmith in the city.

Caludreth went to his knees and spread his hands, holding the shackles against the cobbles.

The blacksmith knelt down, hammer in one hand and a chisel in the other. Mighty blows rang out, and sparks flew in the smoky air.

Menendil glanced back. Chaos had broken out, the soldiers were fighting for their lives, but many of the Hundred concentrated their efforts on the knight. He was the greatest threat, and at any moment he might disengage from those he battled and cast magic at Caludreth. All of this would have been for nothing if the man died now.

There was another mighty hammer blow from the smith, and Caludreth cried out in pain. Menendil glanced down and he saw blood on the cobbles, but the shackles had come free.

"To the horse, my lord!"

He had to help Caludreth stagger up, and then he mounted the horse, pulling the man up behind him. Once more he blew the horn, and it signaled the attack could cease. Now all the Hundred, those still alive, could flee. They would cast away their white arm bands and disappear down the alleys from which they had come.

But even as he did so, he saw that the archers had been forced to flee and soldiers were pouring out of the barracks.

Escape was no longer certain, but even if they did pursuit was guaranteed. It had taken too long to free the prisoner.

22. Shadows

Winter deepened around the mountain, and the plateau was capped by snow. This ran down the slopes also, but it thinned quickly.

It was not as cold here as Faran was used to. Yet the wind blew far more frequently, and harder, and that made it feel colder. It was also more dangerous, and the quickly changing weather atop the mountain was even more volatile in winter than it had been in summer.

The short winter days came and went. The long winter nights passed slowly. Faran trained hard, though he had run into, as Kubodin termed it, the wall. It was an apt description, for no matter how hard Faran trained it seemed that improvements in skill only came by tiny increments now.

It was always so, Asana had assured him. The better you became the harder it was to improve. Skill at this level was eked out like a miner digging into a mountain of stone with a blunt handpick.

Ferla had succumbed to the same problem, but not as badly. She had always been nimbler than he was, and faster. She was better at defecting and returning lightning-like ripostes. In this, she improved no more than Faran. But under Asana's training regimen, she grew stronger, and when she chose to use force she struck with shocking power.

It was not her way though. She nearly danced as she sparred, moving with a grace and fluidity that was much like that of Asana himself. In this way she wore down her opponents, but when she had beaten them and moved in for the killing blow she would use techniques then that benefited from strength.

Her two-handed overhead strike in particular was strong. Once, she had hit Faran on the helm harder than she had intended and his head rang for days afterward.

He had not yet run into the wall though with magic. It was a discipline to him so vast and untapped that it seemed he could progress at any number of skills. And he had, surpassing Kareste's expectations and ceaselessly improving at many things.

He could form shields of magic, and commanded lòhren-fire with which to attack. He could summon smoke and mist. The wind he could call, or hold back. Thunder rolled at his uttering of the right word of power, and even lightning came at his asking.

None of this meant he was particularly strong at these skills. For instance, his lòhren-fire was hot, but it was not of that blistering heat that Kareste could summon and which could melt metal. Yet he improved and grew stronger day by day. The skill he aspired to took decades to acquire, Kareste told him. Or a lifetime. Many who even possessed the talent in the first place never reached their potential. The training was arduous.

Increasingly, as winter passed, they trained under the mountain. It was rarely now just sword sparring or magic. They had reached a point where in order to be pushed both were combined as a matter of course. He and Ferla would spar, trading blows of the blades and strikes and defenses in magic in a seemingly mad chaos of battle. Yet it was anything but.

Asana became withdrawn. It was as though the winter weighed down on him, or some fear of the future occupied his mind. Kubodin was troubled, and he gazed at his master in vexation. As much as he tried, his friend would give him no clue as to what the problem was.

Kareste had taken to wandering the mountain, even in the depths of winter. Cold held little fear for her, and blizzards that might kill ordinary people were of no account. She merely pulled up her hood and walked abroad where others would seek shelter from the deadly wind.

She, like Asana, was troubled. Faran thought she kept a watch, waiting for their enemies to appear. But there had been no sign of them at all, and surely by now their trail was cold and only an ill chance could reveal them.

Or sorcery. Ferla especially seemed worried by that.

"What powers does the king now possess?" she asked Faran one day while they sat alone by a fire in the underground hall. "Do you think he can scry our presence as legends of old speak of during the elù-haraken?"

"I don't know. Yet if he could, surely he would have sent Lindercroft after us now."

She rubbed her hands together before the flames. "I suppose so. Yet Kareste says his powers will grow as he falls deeper under the influence of the stone."

That was something she had told him too. It could not be otherwise, for the stone was immensely powerful. Yet it needed a person to wield it. The stone, Kareste hinted, lured people to use it by enhancing their powers. They became dependent upon it, and used it more and more. In this way it increased its influence. She spoke of it almost as if it were alive, but that could not be. Whatever the case, the king would become stronger over time. But he would also become more evil, for the shadow of the stone would lie deeper over his mind. He would become outwardly stronger but inwardly weaker, unable to exercise his own will and instead acting on the urges of the stone itself.

"The king grows stronger," Faran agreed with her. "And probably the knights with him. But there are limits to power. Also, they're but a handful of men and they suppress an entire kingdom. That's not a situation that can last. Sooner or later the people will revolt."

Ferla shrugged. "Is it really just the king and the knights, though? There will be others. People with high ambitions but low morals. The foolish, seduced by the words of the king rather than repelled by his actions. Not to mention the greedy, the corrupt and the lawbreakers."

She did not seem to be saying these things at random. It seemed to Faran that her thoughts had long been mulled over.

"I hadn't really thought of it like that. You're right though. The king will have his supporters. Even some who would openly say he is right to use the power of the stone. But in the end, the silent majority will make up the far greater number. When they finally act, they'll overwhelm both the king and his supporters."

"You're right," Ferla agreed. "But what then? It'll end in neighbor fighting neighbor and soldier fighting soldier. Even families fighting family."

Faran had no answer to that. Again, he had the sense that this was something she had deeply pondered. Why she had thought of these issues more than he had, he was not sure. But it was remiss of him. He was glad though that she had. She cared more deeply than he did, and he liked that. He learned how to be a better person from watching her.

He had always wanted to just defeat his enemies and bring justice for the destruction of Dromdruin. But he understood now it had never been that simple. It was not that his ambition to do that was bad, but the rule of an evil king would shadow the land in many ways. He had to be brought down. But what then? The land and its people would need healing.

The fall of the king would be but a first step. Afterward, a new order of knights must be established.

More than ever they would have to live up to their legend of being not just warriors but men of learning and wisdom. They would have to be, as Asana would say, sages.

He understood for the first time why the land needed the knights. Yet more than ever, he felt that role was wrong for him. He had no wish to be the seventh knight. What, if anything, he would do in the future he did not know.

That line of thought made him uneasy. He seldom thought of the future. It was dark and misty to him. Unknowable. Yet he felt it waiting like a crouched predator, ready to pounce unexpectedly.

Winter drew on. After it came spring, and the mountain seemed ready to burst with life. It was still dangerous, and the weather was fickle. Yet some days were glorious, and Faran and Ferla reveled in them, walking the mountain top and the slopes, but never straying too far from home. Glorious as things were, sudden blasts of cold air and sleet were not uncommon.

There was something different about Ferla, but Faran could not identify what it was. She was the same as she had ever been, like an older sister who looked out for him. She made him laugh, and she made him think. But deep within herself she was changing as even the mountain changed around them.

At times there was a look of determination in her eyes that scared him. Mostly, this was when they trained sword against sword. But not always. Sometimes he caught her staring into a fire, but her gaze was hotter than any flame. When he asked her what she was thinking, she would merely smile and the old Ferla was back.

Spring passed. The grass sprang up and grew tall and green. In the gardens on the plateau, fruit trees bloomed and bees hummed in the air. The fruit set. The leaf canopy of the trees grew out. Birds returned to the mountain, and the clouds now threatened less rain and parted often to reveal a dazzling sky, so blue and beautiful that Faran's heart ached.

One evening, just as the sun set in glory and the scattering of high clouds turned pink, they sat and talked on the southern edge of the plateau.

Dusk glided over the land. The world was at peace, and Faran looked at Ferla and knew that she was more beautiful than anything in the world. She was his sun. She was his warmth. She was his peace.

But he said nothing to her, and he cursed his lack of courage.

Night deepened. The stars kindled in the sky, but they were not the only lights. Far, far away in the forest of the elves other lights sprang to life, and almost Faran thought he heard music rise up to the mountain top.

But that was not possible. Unless the mountain itself celebrated the arrival of summer after cold, dark winter.

"They celebrate," Ferla said.

"The elves?"

"Of course. They feel the change in the world as do we, but they are closer, the legends say. They are one with their forest, and they love it. They feel its moods and rejoice as the forest wakes and stirs."

Faran understood how they felt.

Behind them, they heard a noise and turned. But it was only Kubodin. His gaze was on the faraway forest, and there was a longing in his eyes. He, too, sensed the beauty in the world. His gruffness was an act.

"It's a special time of year," Kubodin said. "Not often do the Halathrin light fires in their forest."

Even the man's way of speaking was different now. Perhaps his normal way was an act too.

"Don't they worry that the fires could get out of control and burn through the forest?" Faran asked. Certainly in Dromdruin fires were rarely lit.

"Ha! The Halathrin seldom have accidents. They're like Asana – all careful and full of plans. They don't blink unless they've thought about it first and then double-checked that their first thought was right."

Ferla laughed at that, and she was suddenly the old Ferla that he used to know, free of strain and the determination that so often shaped her expression. And for all that Kubodin seemed dismissive of the Halathrin, Faran was sure he had not come this way by accident. He had come specifically to see the lights.

"Do the Halathrin celebrate every year at the same time?" Faran asked.

"Every year, just the same each time," Kubodin answered. "It lasts for a week."

They watched together for a little while longer. The celebrations would go all night, apparently, but the elves did not need a good night's rest so that they could train hard the next day.

"Time to go," Kubodin said at length. "Dinner is waiting and the air grows chill."

Faran felt it too. It had been so pleasant and warm before, but the nights still grew cold and he began to shiver.

They stood and followed Kubodin. The little man walked with his hand on his axe, and he moved slowly. It was almost like he sensed some sort of danger ahead, and even as Faran thought that a sensation of dread overcame him.

They all slowed, and Kubodin drew out the axe now and looked around carefully.

"What is it?" the little man asked. "Do you sense it?"

Faran knew something was wrong, but he was not sure what. The last time he had felt this way…

"It's an elù-drak!" hissed Ferla.

He knew she was right. That feeling of dread came back to him now. Like a knife slipping into his body, the memory of his first sighting of one of them as he fled Dromdruin burst into his mind. He remembered the fear. He remembered also Aranloth's words that the creatures provoked this in order to make their quarry run and reveal themselves.

But none of them moved. They crouched lower, but resisted the urge to run. From somewhere far above, too high to see, came a dreadful cry. It was answered. And answered again.

They were surrounded. The mountain top was not safe, yet still they saw nothing. This meant, Faran believed, that their exact location was not known.

Kubodin grinned fiercely in the dark, and Faran admired him then. If he were scared, he gave a good show of being excited instead.

"Come," the little man whispered. "To move may reveal ourselves, but there is safety inside the mountain."

He moved into the dark then, holding the axe lightly in one hand and walking with his head to the sky. He would not be taken by surprise.

"Watch the front," Faran asked Ferla, "and I'll watch behind us."

The cries grew closer. Dread prickled Faran's skin, and the palm of his hand that gripped his sword was wet with cold sweat.

Step by step, hugging to the shadows and using trees for cover as best they could, they came to the entrance of the underground halls. Here, the elù-draks seemed concentrated. For the first time, they were visible, yet they circled and wheeled high above. This was no attack. Not yet. It was a warning. They had been found. The enemy knew where they were, and were coming for them. It was intended to strike fear into them.

And it did.

23. Flight!

Menendil kicked the horse into a gallop, and the iron-shod hooves clattered down the street with a growing roar.

He bent down low in the saddle. This would make him a smaller target for archers, if there were any among the soldiers pouring out of the barracks, and a smaller target for sorcery also. This was what he feared most.

Caludreth slumped behind him, but his arms still had enough strength in them to wrap around Menendil and hold himself in the saddle.

It was mayhem everywhere. People were running and screaming and shouting. The Hundred were dispersing, but there were soldiers streaming out onto the street as well. A group made for Menendil.

With a pull on the reins Menendil tried to veer out of the way, but the soldier got there first, drawing swords and shouting to try to stop the horse. Perhaps they knew who rode behind him, or perhaps it was coincidence.

To be captured was to die. Menendil urged the horse forward and thundered toward them. Suddenly, the noise of those hooves was intensified. Magic, Menendil knew at once. Caludreth, nearly falling out of the saddle was trying to help.

And it partly worked. Between the rushing of the horse which was enough to scare most men, and the rolling thunder of its approach, most of the soldiers scattered. But a few held their ground and they tried to bring him off the horse.

Menendil's sword was out, and he slashed and hacked. A blade cut him across the stomach, but it was a glancing strike and ill timed. Hands reached up for the reins.

The soldiers were trying to capture both riders. They *knew* who the man behind him was, and they were desperate.

But not as desperate as Menendil. He hacked at the hands trying to bring him and Caludreth down, and then suddenly they were through and onto the clear street again.

To the right, an alley opened up and he turned the horse down it. This was part of his plan.

The horse sped ahead, frightened by the tumult and bolting. Menendil feared it would fall in the dark, slipping on cobbles or shouldering a wall in the narrow passage and throwing both riders to their deaths.

But somehow they came through to the next street. It was quiet here, though many of the Hundred were sprinting away in one direction or the other. Their job was done, and they had done it well. Yet Menendil's was not over.

He turned the horse to the left, and Caludreth nearly slipped off. But then he righted himself and they were away. The soldiers were nowhere in sight, but Menendil could not be sure. He dared not turn and look behind him for more than a passing glance.

The streets were quiet now. The Hundred had slipped away. The soldiers were in pursuit no doubt, but they would be too slow to find any but stragglers. But there seemed to be none of those. The men had fought bravely, but when the time to run had come they had embraced it and reacted more quickly than their enemies. Likely, the fear of more archers and a trap slowed the soldiers.

They came to another corner. Here several riders were gathered, and a lone man on foot. This also was part of Menendil's plan.

Quickly he dismounted in the deep shadows of a tall building, helping Caludreth to do so as well.

"The way is clear!" the lone man said. Then he took the reins of Menendil's horse and vaulted into the saddle.

The riders shouted and scattered. They were a decoy, and Menendil led Caludreth through a door, locked it with the key he possessed and barred it behind them.

It was pitch black in the room, but Menendil fumbled for the lantern and flint that were on a shelf near him.

"Who *are* you?" whispered Caludreth.

The man's voice was hoarse, but for all that he had been through there was no fear in it.

"A friend," Menendil answered. "One of many. But there'll be time for talk later. We yet have work to do, if you can manage it?"

"I can manage," came the answer, "but I hope we don't have far to go."

Menendil got the lantern alight, then put his arm around Caludreth to support him.

"It's not far, my lord. Then you can rest and recover."

They moved through the empty building. It was a potter's warehouse, used to store his goods for distribution through this part of the city, and he was a friend of Menendil's. As had their fathers been friends before them, and back into antiquity some sort of association had always existed.

Menendil found the secret trapdoor built into the floor, and helped Caludreth down. This was difficult, for the man struggled to find his balance on the ladder. It was no surprise, for he could barely see through his swollen eyes and his legs were weak. Every movement also caused him pain.

When they were safely at the bottom, Menendil climbed back up and closed the door, pulling it tightly shut. It was near impossible to find, but that was no guarantee of safety. Outside, he heard a commotion of rushing soldiers.

He waited briefly until they had passed before rejoining Caludreth at the bottom of the ladder. The safety of this plan lay mostly in not being seen entering the building in the first place. Had there been soldiers within view, they would have ridden on toward another place of safety.

They were in a cellar. Even here, there were old tables covered by pots, and it was a dingy place, cluttered by old cobwebs and with dust in the air.

Menendil helped the once-knight forward, and they walked carefully, avoiding the odd pot that had fallen and broken on the floor. It was a cellar, but it was also more than that.

The room narrowed, and now they were pressed tight together. Really, there was only room for one to walk at a time, but Menendil was not sure his companion could manage it. They were now in a passage, and the cellar was behind them.

"We must be under the road?" Caludreth asked.

For all that he had been bashed and beaten, the man had lost none of his wits.

"Indeed. We're at least ten feet below it, as far as I've ever been able to estimate. The tunnel was built in antiquity. It joins the Bouncing Stone Inn, the establishment I own, with the building we just left. It was used in ages past when some king, I forget which, decided it was a good idea to tax the sale of barrels of beer. So the inn, ah, shall we say, had necessity to transport the kegs more privately than by the front entrance which was often watched."

Caludreth chuckled, and then he coughed. "That was King Boraleas. He was a great grandson of the first king, and history remembers him poorly. But I bless his name tonight. Because of him, this tunnel was made."

They came to a door. Three times Menendil knocked on it, and then there was a long pause. Eventually it opened, and Norla stood before them, a knife in her hand.

Her face was flushed with relief. "Welcome home, Mender." It sounded like a simple greeting, but he heard the strain in her voice and knew how much she had worried for him.

Menendil wanted to hug her, but Caludreth needed help, and quickly.

"He's been badly beaten," he said.

Her eyes shifted to their guest. In one glance, she took him in.

"He'll live, but a bit of attention won't go astray."

Caludreth somehow managed a graceful bow, though he grimaced in pain as he did so.

"Madam, you make *a bit of attention* sound like the greatest pleasure in Faladir at just this moment."

She winked at him. "If you can bow and compliment, you'll certainly live. But let's see if we can make you more comfortable."

There was a bed set up in the cellar. Menendil liked to nap there sometimes while he prepared ingredients for a brew, but tonight it would see a nobler purpose.

They led Caludreth to lie down on it, and Norla busied herself assessing the man's health. She had worked for a healer long ago, and she knew some of the trade. It was the best Caludreth could get because they dared not send for the local healer.

"Three of my ribs are broken," Caludreth said. "But I'll recover."

"You had better," Norla answered. "After what my husband risked for you."

Caludreth laughed. "I will. And I'll be forever in his debt. And yours. And the men who fought out on the streets."

They cleaned him up then, as best as they could. They used wet cloths to remove the dried blood from his face, and they bandaged several of his wounds. It seemed the soldiers had been free with knives on him also, though no cut was deep. They had been careful to keep him alive for the king.

Last of all they wrapped a wide bandage about his ribs, and gave him a mug of their strongest ale and half a loaf of bread. He ate and drank as though he had done neither for days, which was probably the truth.

"Rest well for the remainder of the night," Menendil said. "But tomorrow, before my workers return, we'll get you into a room upstairs. You'll be more comfortable there."

Caludreth slept then, perhaps for the first time in days. But Menendil remained on guard. He set himself on a chair near the door to the tunnel and waited.

Dawn was not that far off. Every moment that passed without soldiers bursting in made it more likely that somehow they had gotten away with this undetected. The Hundred had rescued a prisoner of the king, and escaped.

Tomorrow, word would spread like fire through the city. It would give people hope. It would spark unrest, perhaps even rebellion. If the king could be defied in one way, he could be defied in others. For all his dark powers, he was not invincible.

There was a reverse side to it too. The king would see this happening, and he would move to stamp it out. He would be ruthless, and he would seek to find people, guilty or not, and make an example of them to cower the citizens of Faladir. Or he might do something else. But whatever he did, it would be designed to increase his power.

Menendil looked over at where the once-knight slept. Could this man help? Could he be more than a symbol of defiance? Did he have answers to their problems?

Menendil knew that he, himself, did not.

24. Ancestors

Asana sat in the High Chair, and he pondered the future. At least, what remained of it.

He knew he was going to die, and soon. His foretellings never lied, and he remembered the sorcery being cast at him that would take his life. He had no defense. Perhaps, he could have averted that destiny by refusing to train Ferla and Faran. Perhaps. Yet he had not, and he was glad that he had not.

They were the best pupils he had ever taught, and that included some of the great warriors among the Cheng. More than that, they were good people, and their cause was righteous. Moreover, he owed Aranloth much, and the old man would have wanted it so.

But his pondering now was in vain. He had made his choice, and the consequences were inevitable. More than that, he had seen the signs in the foretelling and knew the indicators of when the dark day would come.

It was at hand. He knew it. Fate ran even the fastest runner down, and eternity was but the blink of an eye. He would die, and there was nothing he could do to prevent it.

Yet he could prepare for it. He could do what many of his ancestors had done. There was a ceremony he could perform, one which he had never considered before, but that he had known he would enact from the moment of his foretelling. He had *seen* himself in that vision, even as he sat here now in the High Chair, and with Kubodin going to fetch Faran and Ferla.

He sighed, and turned to Kareste. "Destiny approaches, and there is something I must do. On no account interfere, I beg you."

She looked at him, and there was no surprise on her face. Was that just lòhren poise, or had she seen her own visions?

"I'll not interfere, but what you contemplate cannot be reversed. Are you sure it is your will?"

How she knew what he intended amazed him. But the knowledge of lòhrens ran deep, and he merely accepted that it was so.

"I do as I must, and as I feel is right."

He drew his sword. It was an old weapon, handed down through generation after generation of his ancestors. The metal was both hard yet somewhat flexible. It was as a man's life should be. Unyielding where it came to defying evil, greed, corruption, intimidation and the ill chances of the world. Yet pliant enough to withstand the forces that raged against it and still stand up again afterward.

He uttered the sacred words, and they filled the chamber, whispering back to him. Or perhaps they were no longer his own words but the words of his ancestors, for he had summoned them.

The room grew cold. All about him he sensed the presence of those who had formed him in ages past. He was one with them, and they one with him. Some part of their spirit was bound to the blade, and would never be released until the blade broke.

Even as they had done in their lives, binding themselves by the sacred rite to the sword, so he would do now himself.

It was not immortality. Some held that it would be a torment. He was not sure of that, but he knew it was fitting. He had a destiny, and it involved the sword. When he died, Kubodin had instructions to take the blade, if he could, and find a worthy master to pass it on to. That way Asana could still, in some manner, fulfill his destiny.

The spirits of the sword had little power. But he felt them gather round him now and give him strength. In that, they were influential. It was the power of the mind that governed a person's achievements, and if it were strong there were few limits to what might be done. And the spirits of the dead could offer wisdom and insight to help a person and direct their passions.

So it was that they came to him in dreams. Even, perhaps, they were the source of his foretellings. They were not visible in reality though, but it was said they appeared at the death of one who joined his spirit to the blade.

That, he would discover shortly. He uttered more of the incantation, and as a part of that he sprang forward, for gestures were part of the spell. In this case the gestures were a special sword pattern, and he flowed across the floor, the blade hissing as he struck the air, performing techniques that he knew but in an order that he never dared perform at any other time.

Nor would he ever perform the pattern again.

When he was done, he bowed and then straightened, running the sharp edge of the blade as gently as he could across his left palm. The blood sizzled on the blade, but it did not evaporate. Instead, it seeped into the metal becoming one with it. He had not expected that, but the ceremony had only been handed down to him in whispers.

He swayed, and felt suddenly weak. But then strength filled him again. The ceremony was done, and he was one with the blade and one with his ancestors.

Sheathing the sword, he sat back down on the High Chair.

"A strange magic," Kareste said. "But ancient. The dead are free for a time, but not just in the blade. Nor were all summoned by you."

What she meant, Asana did not know. But her staff was in her hand, and she gripped it tightly. She was ready to fight.

Outside, he heard a fell cry tear apart the night. It came from a great distance, perhaps high in the sky. But it was no natural bird or animal that he had ever heard before.

25. The Seventh Knight

Faran paused. There was movement at the entrance to the underground halls.

A moment later, he breathed a sigh of relief. It was Asana, and beside him was Kareste.

Kubodin went in first, and then Faran and Ferla close behind.

"Elù-draks," Faran warned.

Asana did not look surprised, but there was a grim cast to his face.

"We know," the master replied. For some reason there was a slight cut on his left palm, and a trace of blood on his trousers. He was normally so neat that Faran found it disturbing.

"How do they keep finding us?" Ferla asked.

Kareste peered out of the entrance, but did not step outside.

"It was inevitable. Your enemies will never give up. That, you already know. But how exactly they did it, there's just no way to know. Lòhrens aren't the only ones who have foretellings and visions. Sorcerers do too. Perhaps the stone sensed us somehow. Perhaps the king used some spell. But magic is unreliable for this. Most likely, it was just bad luck. If you look long enough, you'll find what you seek."

It seemed like more than bad luck to Faran. It was the worst luck possible. Then again, they had been here a long time. It just seemed so short looking back on it.

"The question," Kareste continued, "is this. Now that we are found, what are we going to do?"

Faran glanced at Asana and Kubodin. "I'm sorry that we've brought this on you."

Kubodin laughed. "Sorry? Why should that be? I'm looking forward to this! It's going to be the best fight ever!"

At that, Asana smiled. "Do not fear, Faran. I wouldn't change anything. Remember that. I have taught you that in the lands of the Cheng a warrior is also a sage, and that a sage accepts the shifting tides of fate as a matter of course. Destiny is neither sought out nor run from. It's *taken*." He glanced at Ferla as he said those last words, and it seemed at that moment that he would say more. But just then another cry came from the dark sky.

When it ended, Ferla spoke. "Kareste is right. What do we do now? Flee or fight?"

There was a long silence. Ferla looked at him, and he thought he read her intentions.

"Is fleeing an option?" he asked.

Kareste leaned on her staff. "It might be possible. But we're on a mountain here, and there is no escape but down the slopes. They'll be watched by elù-draks, and even magic will struggle to deceive their eyes. Any fighting we do if discovered, will also be out in the open."

"Better to fight here," Kubodin said. "This tunnel is the only way in, and it's narrow. We can defend ourselves here better than anywhere else."

Faran looked at Ferla again. "I think it's time to make a stand. I'm done being hunted. It makes me sick. For good or ill, I want to carry the fight back to our enemies. But we all have to agree to that. We have to stay together because that's our best chance of surviving. So I'll stay here, or try to flee, if that's what we decide to do as a group."

"It's time, Faran," Ferla said. "I too am done running. Live or die, I'm ready to stand against evil."

Faran looked at the others. "What do you all say?"

"Stay and fight," Asana answered.

"Stay and fight," Kareste agreed.

Kubodin grinned. "Kill them all, I say," and he drew his axe out and shook it.

So it was that they stayed, and Faran knew that it would be the longest night of his life and that the world would be changed by the next morning. If he saw it.

There was no need for an elaborate plan. They would defend the narrow tunnel, and if necessary fall back. If they came to the central hall below, they would make their last stand there.

Faran thought about fetching his bow. He had not practiced much with it since coming to the mountain, but he had not neglected it either. Yet the tunnel was narrow, and the opportunities to use it would be limited. What was coming was a job for swords.

They ate a subdued meal, waiting for the enemy. At least they all seemed subdued, except for Kubodin who ate his food with relish.

It was in the middle reaches of the night that the enemy came. It was not what Faran was expecting.

Lindercroft led the enemy, which he had anticipated. He had perhaps twenty men with him also. Some carried smoking torches, and this Faran had expected. But there were other creatures with them, dimly seen in the flickering light, and all dark things of legend. Elugs, which some called goblins, marched in a group by themselves. There were Lethrin too, which were often called trolls. There was a lumbering creature as well, seemingly part lizard and part serpent, but as large as a bull. It was not a dragon, that much Faran knew. But he had no name for it.

Nor was that all that was surprising. Apart from Lindercroft and the men, the other creatures were dead.

They were rotting, their flesh hanging in strips and the battle wounds that had killed them obvious. Faran nearly vomited.

Lindercroft came close to the narrow entrance, walking ahead of his force. Asana stood there, calm and poised. He had possession of the hall, so it was fitting that he was their first spokesperson.

"You, I do not know," Lindercroft said. "But I see those I seek behind you. Give them up to me, or die. That is your choice. If you do so, I have no quarrel with you, and you will suffer no harm."

It seemed to Faran that he meant it, but there was no telling with Lindercroft.

"They are my friends, all of them," Asana replied. "You have no business here. If you attempt to take them, I will stand in your way and you will die."

"I don't know who you are," Lindercroft replied. "And I care less that you carry a sword. But you will not kill me. You don't have the skill. No one does."

Asana grinned in the dim light of the lanterns in the tunnel.

"I did not say that I would be the one to kill you. As to skill, we will see what you think of that by the end."

Lindercroft gave a curt nod, but did not reply. Instead, he walked back to his forces.

Faran glanced at Kareste. "Are the creatures with him illusion?"

She did not take her gaze off the enemy. "No. They're real. Lindercroft has summoned dead from the battlefields near here, and his power is great to do so. And greater still to summon so many. But not so great that he could properly restore their bodies, even for a short time. The stone has lent him great power, but he is not invincible."

"And the dead creatures?" Asana asked.

"Steel can destroy the sorcery just as it can destroy life."

The first attack came soon after. Lindercroft did not fight, himself. His tactic would be to send his forces in first, and perhaps lend them sorcerous aid. Against this, Kareste held herself back. She was best positioned to counter magic.

Asana held the narrow entrance. There was room enough only for one to fight here, and he had charge of these halls and the first duty to protect them.

The master barely seemed to move. His sword arced and curved gracefully, and his strokes appeared unhurried. Yet the elugs which Lindercroft sent first fell before him like leaves blown in the wind.

But there were many of them, and as soon as one fell another took its place. The stench of rotting flesh was nauseating, and the moans of the creatures disturbing. It seemed that they could not speak, and Faran guessed that while sorcery commanded their bodies, the spirits that once gave them life were not present. That meant that Lindercroft controlled and sustained them. If so, he would have little capacity to attack.

The dead piled up before Asana, and as steel severed the magic that bound them to Lindercroft they turned back to the dust and fragments of bone that they had long since been on the battlefield below the mountain.

Unexpectedly, Asana stumbled. At last a sword of the enemy endangered him, and falling backward from the narrow entrance two elugs forced their way in.

Kubodin leaped forward with his axe. That had been arranged. He and Asana knew each other well, and fought in harmony together. They would do so, and when they needed rest Faran and Ferla would take their places.

The wicked axe of Kubodin smashed into the chest of the elug pressing forward against Asana, and this gave the master time to catch his footing again. A moment later Asana's blade sliced through the creature's leg, toppling it.

The enemy pressed hard, driven from behind by Lindercroft. But the two men held their ground, the axe heaving and swiping and the thin blade both flashing death in different ways.

They fought differently too. Kubodin battled like a crazy man, grunting and laughing, even at times taunting his opponents. This he soon stopped when they did not answer back. Instead, he yelled over their heads and called Lindercroft a coward for not fighting himself, and insulted the soldiers with Lindercroft in language that seemed startling even in the midst of battle. But for all that, his axe was deadly.

Asana barely seemed to move, just flowing silently with sublime grace from one technique to the next, executing them as though he were in no hurry at all. Yet his blade flashed quicker than the eye could properly follow, and the heads of long-dead elugs toppled to the floor. Hands fell as well, for the master was disadvantaged by a lighter blade so he used it to its strength. It was sharper than any razor and he sought the most vulnerable points of the enemy – the neck where a gap existed between helmet and chainmail coat, and the hand that held the weapon.

Faran could not imagine two fighters who were more different, yet they both dealt out destruction equally. It seemed that Kubodin only fought at his best in real battle, and now he revealed himself a master of the axe as much as Asana was a master of the blade.

But they were not gods of war, and as good as they were they began to tire for there seemed no end to the enemy. Gradually, they were pushed back.

Faran looked at Ferla. It was their turn, and fear ran through his veins and turned his bones cold. But this was what he had trained for.

"Fall back, Kubodin," he cried.

The little man swung a vicious sideways strike at an elug, smashing its helm away and shattering the skull under it, which was half white bone and half decomposing flesh. Even as it fell he retreated and Faran leaped into the gap.

He faced his first enemy. It was an elug. It had no helm or armor, but it carried a massive mace, pitted and rusted on the surface. This it swung at Faran.

A moment he froze, fear seizing up his limbs. Then he dodged, and felt a rush of air above his face. He moved into The Swallow Dips Low, his sword slicing into the enemy's knee.

The elug staggered and fell, but it was not done fighting. Moaning, it swung its mace again, this time at Faran's own legs.

Faran nimbly jumped the attack, and from his position of height brought down the tip of his sword in Hawk Folds its Wings. The point of the blade penetrated the skull and killed the creature instantly. It spasmed and lurched, then collapsed to the floor. But Faran's blade was stuck in the bone and did not come free when he pulled at it.

Another elug leaped at him, small but fast, and it swung a sickle-shaped blade at his neck. Faran waited until the last moment, then ducked low beneath the attack and pressed forward bringing his left knee up into the creature's groin.

The elug fell back, and the skull in which Faran's sword was stuck crumbled into fragments as the magic that had gathered the corpse together and animated it unraveled.

He darted forward, slashing the elug before him several times until it burst apart in a spray of ancient dust and scattered bones.

Beside him he glimpsed Ferla, neatly killing an elug herself. She was not as strong as him, but she fought with agility and ease, reminding him of Asana. If she felt the fear that Faran had, it did not show.

Two fresh opponents lumbered forward, but they were not elugs. They were Lethrin, towering above him and massive. In their mighty hands were axes, and though he knew techniques that pitted a sword against an axe, he had never faced an opponent before that dwarfed him in size.

But he did not flinch. He would fight, no matter what Lindercroft sent against him.

"For Dromdruin!" he cried, and he darted forward. His sword swept up, but at the last moment he checked himself. It was a feint, and it drew the reaction he wanted.

The Lethrin swung out with his axe. It was a blow intended to sever Faran in half, and it would have if he had gone through with his attack. Instead, he was positioned to strike down on the massive wrist of the creature that was now exposed.

Ancient steel, infused with sorcery, struck the long-dead flesh of a creature raised from the void. There was a dull thud, for hitting the Lethrin was like hitting a tree. But the hand severed from the arm, and the axe went flying to scrape and clatter across the floor.

The Lethrin recoiled and moaned, lifting high its head and venting its anguish. Reacting fast, Faran made his next move. With or without a weapon, this thing could still kill him.

He dropped down low, and then drove up his sword with all the power of his legs and arms. The tip of the blade struck the creature's lower abdomen, and there it met with great resistance. The hide of the troll was like armor. But the point bit, sinking in, and Faran drove higher and higher, pushing up until he felt the blade come clear out his enemy's back.

The troll stiffened, and maggots poured out of the open wound. Faran kicked out, pushing the creature back with his foot while at the same time withdrawing his blade.

The Lethrin thrashed and toppled. Too late Faran pulled the blade free and tried to leap back. The full weight of his enemy fell upon him, and it was like a mountain collapsing.

Then it was gone, the magic unraveling, and he was covered in a mound of dust and massive bones. He tried to stand, but the breath was knocked from him, and an elug skittered toward him over the debris.

Lòhren-fire flared, streaming from Kareste's staff, and the elug writhed momentarily in flames before it too was gone.

Faran was on his feet again, and he glanced toward Ferla and saw that she had killed her own troll. But Lindercroft, somewhere in the midst of the enemy back up the tunnel, answered the intervention of magic with his own.

Choking smoke rose up from the floor, but with a word of power Faran drove it up the tunnel and at the enemy. They fell back, blinded.

"Nice work," Ferla complimented him.

Her red hair had spilled out from beneath the rim of her helm, and dust and grime covered her. But she had never seemed so beautiful.

There was a momentary pause in the battle, and then the enemy rushed forward again.

So the battle wore on. The enemy seemed numberless, but they could only attack two at a time. The defenders held the tunnel, but they were forced back, grudging step by grudging step.

As the battle flowed and ebbed, they continued to swap places to allow themselves some momentary rest. Despite the enemy, they yet all lived, though twice Faran had nearly died and once Asana had only just escaped impalement on a Lethrin spear. This did not reflect their skill, but was just the luck of battle.

But they were all wounded. Faran bled from a gash to his right forearm. It throbbed with pain, but the bleeding had stopped due to a bandage that Kareste had applied while he rested. She herself had just managed to avoid a spear thrown at her, but it had still glanced across her shoulder and drawn blood. Asana and Kubodin had both received cuts to their bodies, but neither was fatal.

Faran had lost track of time. It must be nearing daylight outside, yet in the tunnel there was only the flickering light of the lanterns and the torches of the enemy. His arms were heavy, and his sword-strokes slower than they had been. Some beast came at him, part wolf and part man. It was a creature of dark legend, and it used no blade nor weapon, but fought with fang and claw.

Even when Faran had severed the head from its body, it still came at him with its claws. Ferla saved him then, disengaging from the elug she fought to stab the chest of the creature. In doing so, she had made herself vulnerable and the elug's blade smashed against her helm, raising a shower of sparks.

Faran slashed at the elug, and so did Ferla. It fell in a whirl of ancient dust and rattling bones. But once more they were pushed back as other enemies came at them.

On the battle went, and they had to swap more often for their tiredness grew apace. They could not go on much longer. Nor was there much of the tunnel left. They had come close to the central chamber now. Asana and Kubodin were fighting, and with a hiss something rushed at Kubodin.

It was the creature they had seen briefly before, part lizard and part serpent. Its mighty jaw was agape, and venom dripped from its wicked fangs. Long coils of its body trailed behind it, and it rose up on these to tower above the little man, its head brushing the ceiling. Yet there were legs beneath its body, and these ended in twisted claws.

"It's a dhrokuhl!" warned Kareste. "It can only be killed by magic. Step back and swap with me!"

Kubodin merely laughed. Then he launched himself in fury at the creature. His axe swung, attempting to sever the creature's head from its neck, but it recoiled and the blow missed. Striking forward like a snake, jaw wide and fangs dripping venom, the dhrokuhl retaliated.

Dropping low, Kubodin raised the axe before him like a shield. Fangs struck metal with a screech, and venom spurted over the twin blades.

From the metal, smoke rose. So too did Kubodin. He leaped up as the dhrokuhl drew back in preparation to attack again, but the little man was on it. His axe cut and swung and hacked in killing strokes.

But none of them had much effect. This was a creature of the dark, some monster of legend rarer but more powerful than trolls or even elù-draks.

Kubodin was not dismayed. He laughed all the harder and was still laughing as one of the legs of the creature ripped its claws across his chest. The rags he wore for clothes were rent, and blood seeped into the tattered remnants. Yet still the little man fought on. But he laughed no more.

With a curse that rang through the tunnel, Kubodin struck back. Again and again his axe bit into flesh, but it caused no real damage. But even as the little man fought, he began to chant.

The language was strange and guttural. Faran did not know what it was, but it was no longer a curse. He stepped forward to help, if he could, but Kareste held him back.

"Wait!" she cried. "And watch!"

Faran did not know what was happening, but he sensed magic. Kareste must have felt it before him. Kubodin's chanting was some kind of spell, and even as he kept swinging the axe it seemed to glow with a strange orange light, as though the metal of the blades was being reforged in a smith's furnace.

Again and again, Kubodin hacked at the dhrokuhl. It spat venom at him, but this ignited in the air like dry leaves on a fire as the axe-blades passed through it.

With one mighty stroke, Kubodin severed the head from the body. It clattered against the floor and the jaws went still, but the body writhed and twisted even as it burst into flame.

Fire roared in the tunnel like a furnace, and Kubodin staggered back, his hair singed, but he grinned. Asana reeled away with him, his expression, for the first time that Faran had ever seen, one of utter amazement.

"You possess magic?"

Kubodin grinned harder, but did not answer.

When the flames died down, there were no more creatures of the shadow. Only men remained, and Lindercroft behind them. But those men now held the entrance, for the defenders had fallen back into the central hall.

Lindercroft came forward. He was a figure of awe, wearing the armor of a Kingshield Knight, and there was power in his gaze.

"I have waited long for this," he said. "We are far away from Dromdruin, but what was begun there will end here."

"It will end," Kareste answered. "But not as you wish it. You have only twenty men left."

Lindercroft turned his cold gaze to her. "But they are twenty *fresh* men, and you are all wounded and exhausted.

And I am a knight, granted power beyond your imagination by the king."

Leaning on her staff, Kareste laughed. "You are a fool Lindercroft. The king has no power. None. All he has and all he gives now comes from the Morleth Stone. And it will not be enough. It was not at the founding of Faladir, nor will it be enough here."

Lindercroft looked thoughtful. "You say that, now. You act brave, *now*. Even so did Aranloth. But at the end he was a coward. He screamed for mercy and begged for his life. But screams and begging availed him naught. I silenced the first and took joy in the second. So I shall do with you." He cast his gaze around the room. "So I shall do with all of you, and you will wish you had not been born."

Silence fell heavily over the room. The only sound was the shuffling boots of the enemy soldiers. They, at least, did not seem so confident as their master.

Faran felt anger rise within him. But he did not believe Lindercroft's words. He was a liar. Aranloth was no coward.

At a signal from Lindercroft, his soldiers suddenly attacked. They rushed at the smaller group of defenders, seeking to overwhelm them with their numbers. But numbers alone were not a substitute for skill.

Steel rang against steel. Kubodin's axe cleaved a head off a soldier, the first one to go down. But Asana killed a man a moment later, spilling his bowels onto the floor, and both Faran and Ferla killed men too. To lose so many of their number so fast must have sent a chill of fear into those who remained, but they only attacked all the more desperately. No doubt, they knew if they tried to pull back Lindercroft would kill them, and they feared him even more.

They had reason to. Raising his left hand, crimson fire dripped from his fingers. Lòhren-fire struck at him, brilliant blue in the dim chamber. Against this he contemptuously raised a shield of sorcery, and flung his fire at the defenders.

Lindercroft was grown greater than he had been before. Once, Kareste would have defeated him in a battle of magic, but now he was above her. Or rather, the Morleth Stone gave him that power. Faran could feel some connection between man and stone, and even as he glanced at Lindercroft's eyes, he knew he was looking also into the heart of the stone itself, for his enemy's gaze was like two black pits of evil.

The sorcerous fire scattered and spread. Against it, Faran and Ferla raised their own shields. Kubodin and Asana leapt out of the way. The defenders were safe, this time. But one of Lindercroft's own men went down, writhing and screaming as the red fire shriveled his face and turned his hair into a gruesome torch.

Kareste ran forward, charging against Lindercroft with her staff before her and lòhren-fire flaring. She smashed into his shield, thrusting her staff into it and blinding light flared, accompanied by a mighty boom. The floor heaved. Rubble fell from the ceiling. Both her and Lindercroft were thrown through the air.

Kareste fell, rolled, and then lay still, her staff clattering away from her hand. But slowly, Lindercroft rose.

At that moment, Asana yelled and drew the sorcerer-knight's attention. Crimson fire flared to life again in his hand, and he straightened to his full height.

Even as Lindercroft and Kareste had fought, so the battle with blades continued. But the soldiers were outmatched. They fell and died, and of all the horde that the sorcerer-knight had summoned, only he now stood alive.

But he was a towering figure of rage and power, and his dark eyes shone with the force of the Shadow, black and malevolent. His sword he held in one hand, yet his sorcery was more dangerous. But against whom would he direct it?

Lindercroft cast his gaze around the chamber, and his eyes were maddened by what they saw. His force was destroyed, but his enemies, though tattered and wounded, still stood in defiance. Even Kareste began to stir.

Asana remembered his vision. The moment of death was upon him, and he felt his detachment slipping. He did not want to die. But Ferla and Faran must live. So too Kareste who must yet guide them. And there was also Kubodin, the best friend he had ever had the honor of having.

The knight straightened. The great sword in one hand but sorcerous flame in the other. He could fling it anywhere, but he must assume Kareste his greatest threat. She would be the first to die.

But not if Asana could prevent it. "Die, coward!" he shouted. He was too far away to intervene with his sword, but he slipped a knife out of its sheath and flung it in one swift motion.

Lindercroft battered it away with his sword. It was no real threat, for it would not have penetrated the man's armor, and Asana was too far away to try to hit the throat.

But it drew the knight's ire, which was its true purpose.

Lindercroft raised high his hand, a ball of flame swirling within it, crimson as blood and roiling with sorcerous life. He flung it at Asana with a snarl.

Death hurtled at him. He saw it coming, and the fireball expanded and grew as it tore the air. This was his last moment. He began to leap out of the way despite knowing he could never move fast enough to evade it.

But even as he moved, Kubodin was already running. He chanted as he stepped directly in the path of the sorcery, and held high his axe.

A mighty boom filled the chamber as though thunder rumbled from an angry sky. The earth heaved and shook. Crimson sorcery flared and smashed up into the ceiling, bringing down massive chunks of stone. The axe in Kubodin's hand pulsed like red-hot metal in a smith's forge, then clattered to the floor as Kubodin reeled back and fell.

Asana was stunned. He crashed into the floor, landing badly, but rolled to his feet and ran to his friend. Kubodin had saved him, and he lived against all hope, but the little man lay still.

The sorcerous light was too bright to look at, and when it winked out Faran's eyes could not properly see. But they focused a moment later, and when they did he saw Kareste on her feet, staff in hand. Asana crouching down beside Kubodin, and Ferla engaged in a sword duel with Lindercroft.

He hastened toward Ferla to help, but Kareste grabbed him and held him back.

"No! This is fated. They must fight."

Faran tried to break free, but she held him with an iron grip.

"What if he uses sorcery?"

"He cannot," Kareste answered. "He is spent for a few moments. The fight will be sword to sword, and knight to knight. This is her destiny, Faran. Watch, and be proud of her."

Faran sensed that more was going on here than he knew, but he trusted Kareste, and to try to help Ferla now might only endanger her by breaking her concentration.

The room was still except for swirling dust and the two battling warriors. No one else moved.

Lindercroft struck out, his sword darting in a disemboweling thrust, but Ferla shifted her weight back and avoided it. Even as she had done so often while sparing Faran, she had not really retreated though, and her movement backward merely positioned her to spring forward and attack.

This she did, and her blade swept the air in a glittering arc. Nearly, the tip of it cut Lindercroft's throat, but he staggered back just in time, surprise flaring to life on his face.

Ferla allowed him no respite. She was greatly skilled, and she pressed home her attack moving into Tempest Blows the Dust.

To this, Lindercroft seemed to have no answer. He retreated, swaying as he did so to present a less predictable target. It seemed that Ferla had his measure, and her stepping quickened and her sword strokes cut the air.

Lindercroft stumbled slightly. The point of his sword lowered, but Faran's heart pulsed in his throat. He knew the move. It was Cherry Blossom Falls from the Tree, and it was designed to lure an attacker to be overzealous.

Ferla struck at his head, but at the last moment stifled her stroke. Even at that moment, Lindercroft swayed to the side, and then drove his blade up at her stomach in a killing blow. Such strength was behind it that even Ferla's chainmail might not resist the point of the blade.

But she had seen the trap even as Faran had, and she flung herself backward just in time. She was off balance though, and Lindercroft pursued her eagerly.

At first, there was a great clash of blades as she retreated. Lindercroft pressed as hard as he could to ensure she was not able to regain her poise. Yet she did, and gradually the clanging of blades softened as she began to deflect his strikes rather than block them.

Lindercroft was surprised once more, and then frustrated. At last, anger showed on his face and he renewed his attack with blows of great speed and power.

No longer retreating, Ferla avoided them where she could and deflected where she could not. But she gave up no more ground. Instead, she advanced.

Faran silently willed her on. She was a match for Lindercroft, and the knight knew it and hated it. Forward she advanced, attacking and probing, seeking a weakness in his defenses, and forcing him to retreat.

Lindercroft feinted, moving his shoulder as though he intended a mighty blow, but instead the tip of his blade darted forward at Ferla's throat.

She was not deceived. Swaying to the side, she brought her blade down toward Lindercroft's wrist. It was a blow intended to sever his hand, which was now well forward and exposed. She did not hit flesh, for at the last moment Lindercroft turned his wrist so that the hilt caught the blow. Even so, his sword was jarred from his grip and clattered away over the floor.

Lindercroft did not move. Perhaps he was stunned, or maybe he feared that any movement might trigger Ferla to attack, for she stood before him, the point of her blade poised and ready to strike.

"You are a worthy opponent," Lindercroft said. "I underestimated you. Join with me, and serve the king. He will find a place for you among our order and reward you with powers undreamed of and wealth to beggar nations. I will vouch for you, and you will be as a sister to us."

Ferla tilted her head, as if in thought. "You still have not guessed," she said.

"Guessed what?"

"I am the seventh knight," Ferla replied. "It is my fate, and I am the enemy of you and your brother knights. I would never join you, but I *will* overthrow you."

Ferla seemed like a queen as she spoke, and her words were quiet but hard as cold steel.

"I am the seventh knight, and with my blade I shall cleanse Faladir of evil. I am justice, and I shall slay you and your brother knights. Nor even will the king be spared. He will topple into ruin and fire, and the void will have no mercy on his soul."

Lindercroft's eyes widened in sudden surprise, and then his glance shifted toward his sword that lay on the floor. Even as he moved, so too did Ferla. With great speed she drove the blade forward, striking into his abdomen. She leaned all her bodyweight into the blow, and the sword of the long-dead Letharn queen, smithied at the birth of the Letharn empire and infused with all their skill and magic, burst through the cunningly-wrought links of his chainmail coat and slid up behind his ribs to reach and destroy Lindercroft's heart.

The knight staggered back, and Ferla pulled her blade free. Lindercroft made to speak, but blood frothed at his lips and he collapsed before her, first to his knees and then to the floor.

"I'm sorry, Osahka," he muttered, and then he died.

Faran did not know if he called on Aranloth with his dying breath, or the Morleth Stone. But he *was* dead, and Ferla lived. Her words had stunned him, but they had the ring of truth to them. She was the seventh knight, and that felt right to him.

Pride surged through him. And her eyes met his own, and there was such determination in them that nearly he stepped back.

Kubodin began to laugh, softly at first, and then louder as Asana helped him to his feet.

"A good fight, hey?" he asked.

So it was, too. Somehow, they had all survived, though there were wounds among them that would take weeks to heal. It would take a long time to get used to Ferla as the seventh knight, as well.

Epilogue

Several days after the battle, the defenders were still healing. But they had cleaned the halls of debris and dead. Lindercroft's soldiers they had buried and covered with stones on the northern slope of the mountain, facing toward Faladir. Lindercroft was buried nearby on the plateau, his sword marking his grave.

No one spoke over his resting place, except Kareste. Once, he had been a noble man, she had said, and for that she remembered him.

Faran and Ferla wandered in the gardens afterward, drawing in the beauty at the top of the mountain as a medicine for the horrors they had recently seen. Kubodin rested, laying down on the grass and idly fingering his axe. But Asana and Kareste stood near the entrance to Danath Elbar, talking quietly.

"What happened to the elù-draks?" Asana asked.

Kareste glanced skyward, but there was no sign of them. They had not been seen since the battle.

"It might be that Lindercroft sent them away once we had been located. Or maybe at his death they returned to the king, seeking new instructions. But for now, they are gone."

They watched Ferla reach out and draw a flower blossom toward her to smell its scent, Faran close by her side.

"She fought well," Asana observed.

"Very well. And she has not reached her peak yet."

Asana knew that was true. She was the most gifted student he had ever had, and the confidence gained from defeating a Kingshield Knight would spur her to train even harder.

"When do you think she realized she was the seventh knight?" he asked.

"I think she has known since close to the beginning. Aranloth always suspected it was her rather than Faran. Certainly, it was confirmed in the Tombs of the Letharn."

"And Faran? Do you think he knows his destiny yet?"

Kareste looked at him shrewdly. "Just how much of the future do your visions show you?"

"Enough," he answered.

She was silent a while. "Aranloth had a foretelling concerning him," she said at length. "It may or may not come to pass. But if it does, it will be a greater surprise to him than Ferla's destiny was to her."

Thus ends *The Sage Knight*. The Kingshield series continues in book four, *The Sworn Knight*, where Ferla begins her quest to overcome the evil in Faladir and Faran seeks his own fate, and what secrets it might hold…

THE SWORN KNIGHT

BOOK FOUR OF THE KINGSHIELD SERIES

COMING SOON

Amazon lists millions of titles, and I'm glad you discovered this one. But if you'd like to know when I release a new book, instead of leaving it to chance, sign up for my new release list. I'll send you an email on publication.

Yes please! – Go to www.homeofhighfantasy.com and sign up.

No thanks – I'll take my chances.

Dedication

There's a growing movement in fantasy literature. Its name is noblebright, and it's the opposite of grimdark.

Noblebright celebrates the virtues of heroism. It's an old-fashioned thing, as old as the first story ever told around a smoky campfire beneath ancient stars. It's storytelling that highlights courage and loyalty and hope for the spirit of humanity. It recognizes the dark, the dark in us all, and the dark in the villains of its stories. It recognizes death, and treachery and betrayal. But it dwells on none of these things.

I dedicate this book, such as it is, to that which is noblebright. And I thank the authors before me who held the torch high so that I could see the path: J.R.R. Tolkien, C.S. Lewis, Terry Brooks, David Eddings, Susan Cooper, Roger Taylor and many others. I salute you.

And, for a time, I too shall hold the torch high.

Appendix: Encyclopedic Glossary

Note: the glossary of each book in this series is individualized for that book alone. Additionally, there is often historical material provided in its entries for people, artifacts and events that are not included in the main text.

Many races dwell in Alithoras. All have their own language, and though sometimes related to one another the changes sparked by migration, isolation and various influences often render these tongues unintelligible to each other.

The ascendancy of Halathrin culture, combined with their widespread efforts to secure and maintain allies against elug incursions, has made their language the primary means of communication between diverse peoples.

This glossary contains a range of names and terms. Many are of Halathrin origin, and their meaning is provided. The remainder derive from native tongues and are obscure, so meanings are only given intermittently.

Often, names of Camar and Halathrin elements are combined. This is especially so for the aristocracy. Few other tribes had such long-term friendship with the immortal Halathrin as the Camar, and though in this relationship they lost some of their natural culture, they gained nobility and knowledge in return.

List of abbreviations:

Cam. Camar

Comb. Combined

Cor. Corrupted form

Chg: Cheng

Hal. Halathrin

Leth. Letharn

Prn. Pronounced

Alithoras: *Hal.* "Silver land." The Halathrin name for the continent they settled after leaving their own homeland. Refers to the extensive river and lake systems they found and their wonder at the beauty of the land.

Angle (the): An area of land that formed the heart of the ancient Letharn empire. It begins at their tombs, is hemmed in by two rivers, and rises to a great hill where their capital city was constructed. The ruins of that city remain. Despite the passage of countless years, the streets remain mostly free of growth and the accumulation of dirt that buries other abandoned cities over time. Legend claims that at certain nights of the year the dead Letharn, bound to Alithoras in the tombs, walk in the flesh down the streets they once lived in and the tramping of millions of feet clears the city of dirt and vegetation.

Aranloth: *Hal.* "Noble might." A lòhren of ancient heritage. Travels Alithoras under different names and guises.

Asana: *Chg.* "Gift of light." Rumored to be the greatest sword master in the history of the Cheng people. His father was a Duthenor tribesman.

Balan: *Cam.* "White sand – a beach." A member of the Hundred.

Boraleas: *Cam.* "The glint of green in sunlit seawater." A great grandson of the first king of Faladir. Rumored to have been a gambler and to have emptied the city's coffers. Died as a young man one night in a drunken duel with a stranger.

Bouncing Stone (the): An ancient inn built at the same time as the Tower of the Stone. It is said a smithy occupied the land previously, and here of old attempts were made to destroy the Morleth Stone.

Brand: *Duth.* A heroic figure in Alithoras. Both warrior and lòhren. Stories of his exploits have spread over the land, and they kindle hope wherever they are heard.

Calm in the Storm: The state of mind a true warrior seeks in battle. Neither angry nor scared, neither hopeful nor worried. When emotion is banished from the mind, the body is free to express the skill acquired through long years of training.

Camar: *Cam.* A race of interrelated tribes that migrated in two main stages. The first brought them to the vicinity of Halathar, homeland of the immortal Halathrin; in the second, they separated and established cities along a broad stretch of eastern Alithoras. Faladir is one such city.

Caludreth: *Cam.* "Lord of the waves." A poetic term in Camar literature for a ship.

Cardoroth: *Cor. Hal. Comb. Cam.* A Camar city, often called Red Cardoroth. Some say this alludes to the red granite commonly used in the construction of its buildings, others that it refers to a prophecy of destruction. If so, Brand appears to have thwarted it.

Careth Nien: *Hal.* "Great river." The largest river in Alithoras.

Cheng: *Chg.* "Warrior." The overall name of the various related tribes that dwell in the northwest of Alithoras. It was a word for warrior in the dialect of a tribe that rose to supremacy and set an emperor above all the various clans to unite them.

Cheng Fah: *Chg.* "Warrior arts." Not just warrior arts, but also battle strategy, tactics, medicine, metallurgy and philosophy.

Cheng-mah: *Chg.* "Warriors of perfection." The greatest warriors of any generation. Masters of battlefield arts and philosophy. A sage who is a warrior and a warrior who is a sage.

Danath Elbar: *Hal.* "Underground mansion." Halls delved by the Halathrin into the stone of Nuril Faranar, the mountain used at times as a command post during the Shadowed Wars.

Dhrokuhl: *Hal.* "Rock biter." A creature of the shadow. Not common even during the elù-haraken, but said to lair in the southern mountain ranges of Alithoras amid rubble and fissures from whence it would launch sudden and unexpected attacks against unwary travelers.

Discord: The name of Kubodin's axe. It has two blades. One named Chaos and the other Spite.

Dromdruin: *Cam.* "Valley of the ancient woods." One of many valleys in the realm of Faladir. Home of Faran, and birthplace throughout the history of the realm of many Kingshield Knights.

Druilgar: *Hal.* "Spear star – a comet." King of Faladir, and First Knight of the Kingshield Knights. Descendent of King Conduil.

Drummald Village: *Cam.* "Battle mound." A village of outlaws and fugitives formed amid the ancient battlegrounds of the elù-haraken.

Duthenor: *Duth.* "The people." A tribe of people farther to the west of Camar lands. Related to the Camar, and sharing many common legends and experiences. But different also.

Durnwah: A word of power. It means shield.

Elves: See Halathrin.

Elù-drak: *Hal.* "Shadow wings." A creature of the dark. Deadly, and used by sorcerers to gather information and assassinate chosen victims. The female of the species is the most dangerous, having the power to inspire terror and bend victims to her will. Few can resist. Of old, even great warriors succumbed and willingly let the creature take their life. One of the more terrible creatures of the Old World.

Elugs: *Hal.* "That which creeps in shadows." A cruel and superstitious race of goblins that mostly inhabit the southern lands of Alithoras. Also found in the far north.

Elùgai: *Hal. Prn.* Eloo-guy. "Shadowed force." The sorcery of an elùgroth.

Elù-haraken: *Hal.* "Shadowed wars." Long ago battles in a time that is become myth to the scattered Camar tribes.

Faladir: *Cam.* "Fortress of Light." A Camar city founded out of the ruinous days of the elù-haraken.

Faran: *Cam.* "Spear of the night – a star." A name of good luck. Related to the name Dardenath, though of a later layer of linguistic change. A young hunter from Dromdruin valley. His grandfather was a Kingshield Knight, though not the first of their ancestors to be so.

Ferla: *Cam.* "Unforeseen bounty." A young hunter from Dromdruin valley.

First Knight: The designated leader of the Kingshield Knights.

Halath: *Hal.* Etymology unknown. A lord of the Halathrin who led his people into Alithoras.

Halathar: *Hal.* "Dwelling place of the people of Halath." The forest realm of the Halathrin.

Halathrin: *Hal.* "People of Halath." A race of elves named after an honored lord who led an exodus of his people to the land of Alithoras in pursuit of justice, having sworn to defeat a great evil. They are human, though of fairer form, greater skill and higher culture. They possess a unity of body, mind and spirit that enables insight and endurance beyond the native races of Alithoras. Said to be immortal, but killed in great numbers during their conflicts in ancient times with the evil they sought to destroy. Those conflicts are collectively known as the Shadowed Wars.

Hundred (the): A resistance group established in Faladir to prepare the way for the coming of the seventh knight.

Immortals: See Halathrin.

Kareste: *Hal.* "Ice unlocking – the spring thaw." A lòhren of mysterious origin. Friend to Aranloth, but usually more active farther north in Alithoras than Faladir.

Kingshield Knights: An order of knights founded by King Conduil. Their sacred task is to guard the indestructible Morleth Stone from theft and use by the evil forces of the world. They are more than great warriors, being trained in philosophy and the arts also. In addition to their prime function as guards, they travel the land at whiles dispensing justice and offering of their wisdom and council.

Kubodin: *Chg.* Etymology unknown. A wild hillman from the lands of the Cheng. Simple appearing, but far more than he seems. Asana's manservant.

Letharn: *Hal.* "Stone raisers. Builders." A race of people that in antiquity conquered most of Alithoras. Now, only faint traces of their civilization endure.

Lethrin: *Hal.* "Stone people." Also called trolls. Creatures of the Shadow. Renowned for their size and strength.

Lindercroft: *Cam.* "Rising mountain crashes – a wave rolling into the seashore." A Kingshield Knight. Youngest of the order.

Lòhren: *Hal. Prn.* Ler-ren. "Knowledge giver – a counselor." Other terms used by various nations include wizard, druid and sage.

Lòhren-fire: A defensive manifestation of lòhrengai. The color of the flame varies according to the skill and temperament of the lòhren.

Magic: Mystic power. See lòhrengai and elùgai.

Menendil: *Hal.* "Sign of hope." Sometimes called Mender. His is an old family, and he can trace his lineage back to the days before the founding of Faladir to a liegeman of the then chieftain. Unusually, his name is not of Camar origin. Family history records that his forefather was a seer, and was greatly esteemed by his lord.

Morleth Stone: *Hal.* "Round stone." The name signifies that such a stone is not natural. It is formed by elùgai for sorcerous purposes. The stone is strengthened by arcane power to act as a receptacle of enormous force. Little is known of their making and uses except that they are rare and that elùgroths perish during their construction. The stone guarded by the Kingshield Knights in Faladir is said to be the most powerful of all that were created. And to be sentient.

Nadrak: Etymology obscure, but not of Camar origin. A wool merchant in Faladir who supports the king.

Norgril: *Cam.* "Leaping fish." A member of the Hundred.

Norla: *Cam.* "Fish hunter – fisherman." Wife of Menendil.

Nuril Faranar: *Hal.* "Lonely watchman." A single mountain rising above the flat lands that border Halathar. Used as a vantage point and command post for several great battles during the elù-haraken. Currently under the guardianship of Asana. For this, Aranloth interceded on his behalf.

Osahka: *Leth.* "The guide – specifically a spiritual or moral guide." A title of enormous reverence and respect. Applied to Aranloth for his role as spiritual leader of the Kingshield Knights.

Path of Nature: A philosophy among the Cheng. A follower seeks to be one with the world, understanding the cycles of the universe and trying not to impose human will on the uncontrollable. This can only lead to unhappiness.

Savanest: *Cam.* "Subtle skill." A Kingshield Knight. All the knights think of each other as brothers. But Savanest and Sofanil are also brothers by blood.

Shadow Fliers: See elù-drak.

Shadowed Wars: See elù-haraken.

Sofanil: *Cam.* "Sharp of wits." A Kingshield Knight. All the knights think of each other as brothers. But Sofanil and Savanest are also brothers by blood.

Sorcerer: See elùgroth.

Sorcery: See elùgai.

Tower of the Stone: The tower King Conduil caused to be built to serve as the guarding structure of the Morleth Stone. Some claim his sarcophagus rests upon its pinnacle, as it was the custom of some ancient Camar royalty to be interred on a high place where the lights of the sun, moon and stars still lit their long sleep.

Way of the Sword: The martial aspect of the training of a Kingshield Knight.

Were-beast: A creature of the shadow. Said to be able to shapeshift from animal to human form.

Wizard: See lòhren.

About the author

I'm a man born in the wrong era. My heart yearns for faraway places and even further afield times. Tolkien had me at the beginning of *The Hobbit* when he said, ". . . one morning long ago in the quiet of the world . . ."

Sometimes I imagine myself in a Viking mead-hall. The long winter night presses in, but the shimmering embers of a log in the hearth hold back both cold and dark. The chieftain calls for a story, and I take a sip from my drinking horn and stand up . . .

Or maybe the desert stars shine bright and clear, obscured occasionally by wisps of smoke from burning camel dung. A dry gust of wind marches sand grains across our lonely campsite, and the wayfarers about me stir restlessly. I sip cool water and begin to speak.

I'm a storyteller. A man to paint a picture by the slow music of words. I like to bring faraway places and times to life, to make hearts yearn for something they can never have, unless for a passing moment.

Printed in Great Britain
by Amazon